HAUNTING OBSESSION

A Rebecca Burton Novella

R. J. SULLIVAN

Dedication

DAMN YOU, RODNEY CARLSTROM!! And many thanks, Bro, for your comment that "distracted" me with this project.

And to Sara Larson, who believed in and encouraged writers her entire life, including me. I know that, somewhere, she is doing a fist-pump.

Notes

A note on Maxine: Maxine Marie is an homage to the late, great Marilyn Monroe. I am not the first, nor the last, to be inspired by her tragic life. "Maxine" is a supernatural entity who is overwhelmed by corruptive influences. Maxine's unpleasant nature should not be read as a commentary on Ms. Monroe.

"The Transit King" is the intellectual property of E. Chris Garrison, first featured in her novel *Blue Spirit,* © 2010. All references used with permission. *sillyhatbooks.com*

The author photo features Lily Monstermeat as Maxine, photographed by Silver Sight Photography. R.J. was photographed by Linda Sullivan at Bredensteiner Imaging in Indianapolis, Indiana. Nell Williams combined the components and added effects to create the final image.

Thanks to "Team R.J."

Editor Prime "Doctor Debra" Holland for always riding to the rescue. *debraholland.com*

Michael West and Stephen Zimmer for their faith in my talent; Amanda DeBord for saying "yes" and for bringing her editing skills on the original Seventh Star edition. Bonnie Wasson for her art!

Lily MonsterMeat for embodying Maxine in so many marketing projects, including the incredible standee appearing at a signing event near you! *lilymonstermeat.com*

Nell Williams for offering her awesome 3D art talent whenever I needed it. *nellwilliams.com* Her sister, Nicole Rinaldi, for years of friendship and being such a cheerleader since the beginning.

Jan Pulsford, a.k.a. Athena Blue, one of my music heroes, for contributing the music trailer remix--a collaborative dream come true! *janpulsford.com*

My awesome beta readers

Steve Craig, E. Chris Garrison, Nikki Howard, Kathy Watness, Mary Kay Woolsey, and my "number one fan," Monica A. Felver-Kellogg.

Special thanks to Linda "Mrs. R.J." and Mom and Dad, for your unwavering support.

2020 update

Bryan Donihue for guiding me through this major revision.

YOU ALL ROCK!!

Prologue

1954

JEANIE BRACKEN SNUCK into her apartment and shut the door. She hoped the landlord hadn't heard her come up the stairs. She leaned against the door, breathing in the hot, humid air of unventilated living space. Tiny splinters poked through the thin sundress, pricking her shoulders and back. She looked down at herself, noting with some distress how her yellow sundress clung to her damp skin.

As much as her admirers loved that sort of peek-a-boo look, (and as much as, on certain days, *she* loved how *they* loved that sort of peek-a-boo look) today her breasts hung heavy, a pair of sandbags pulling at her shoulders and draining her strength. Her hair, full and billowing and bleached icy blonde, (all the rage these days, her manager said) hung in wet clumps across her forehead.

Jeanie drew her manicured fingers through her scalp and pushed the strands up and out of her eyes. The mass flopped in a limp wave to one side.

She spied herself in the hall mirror. *You had better be worth it, little miss!* She waved a finger at the image she barely recognized.

For the past month and a half, she'd followed her agent from spa to spa. New hair, new eyelashes, new nails. Then a trip to the state office to make her new name official!

A new name! She said it out loud into the air, still getting used to it. "Maxine Marie." Today's errand toward her transformation also involved a consultation for a surgeon to sculpt a new nose, a procedure scheduled for next month.

Being glamorous really isn't all that glamorous, that's for sure!

She drew another sigh, lifting the bosom that turned so many men's heads, then dragged herself over to the kitchen table and stabbed a finger at a button on the base of the table fan. The blades hummed to life, pushing stale air over her skin. She plopped down into the chair and closed her eyes, letting the blast of air lull her.

Today, she'd returned from her first shoot, and barely had time to hit the bank before...

A knock at the door made her jump.

"Jeanie! Open up! I heard you turn on your fan through the door! I know you're in there."

Crap! She jumped to her feet, stepping toward the door and cracking it open. She spoke to the towering presence looming in the hallway. "Hi, Roger. Is rent due already?"

"No, Jeanie, the rent is not due today. The rent was due last week. And you know it." Roger removed the cigar from his lips and blew a thick cloud of dust at the crack of the door. "I need something, or you're out on your ass."

'I'm sorry, Roger. Hold on a minute."

She shut the door and removed the chain lock. As the door swung open, she chose to ignore how her landlord's angry glare changed to a not-so-subtle leer. "Sorry, Jeanie. I need something. I have expenses, too."

"I know, Roger. How much do I owe?"

"Seventy-five dollars."

"But my rent is sixty-five."

"Your rent is sixty-five when it's on time, Jeanie."

Jeanie opened her checkbook, though she knew perfectly well the damning number recorded in the balance column, *$70.00*

"Roger..."

"Oh, boy, here we go. You're standing there looking not-at-all like yourself, spending all that money on your hair and your nails, and your..." Roger waved his hands in a vague gesture to indicate her body, "...everything else. You know what? I gotta tell ya, you look like a million bucks. And that means you should have my seventy-five."

Jeanie could tell by Roger's tone he wouldn't be put off or hear excuses another day. "Roger, honestly, I can pay you the sixty-five. It's all I have. Look, I posed for a photo shoot today, and I got the advance." As she spoke, she felt the dress's shoulder strap, the one closest to Roger, start to drop to her forearm. She let it, pretending not to notice. "These are ...kinda saucy photos, but still something you can show in public. You know I'm a good girl, don't you, Roger?"

"I know it, Jeanie." Roger's tone softened. "You would have been out on your ass a long time ago if I thought you didn't have no morals."

"I know, Roger, but a girl struggles these days. Someone like me has to turn down some of the jobs out there because they want me to..." She pouted and shrugged, noting how Roger's Adam's apple bobbed in a hard swallow as his imagination surely filled in the variations of requests.

"So when this job finally came along—sexy but *classy* photos, Rog, the kind that are going to take me places. Well, it just happened today. And my agent, he says things will start taking off very soon now."

"Ah, well, okay, I get that. I don't want you getting yourself in trouble just to pay me."

Jeanie smiled, watching him fidget as she lowered her lashes. "Ro-og...if you let me pay you $65.00, I can get a copy of those photos for you to make up the ten bucks. I don't mind. You can even show people. What'cha say?"

"Well, I..." He paused, pretending to think about it, though

Jeanie could see he wanted to jump at the opportunity. "I think that sounds fair enough, Jeanie. If I can collect the cash today."

Jeanie flashed her devastating smile of gratitude. "Thanks, Rog, you're just...just *elegant*." She hopped up onto her feet and leaned forward, and her full lips brushed against the stubble of his cheek and pulled back again.

Roger's face lit bright red. "That's nice of you to say, Jeanie."

"Oh!" Jeanie covered her mouth with her hand and stifled a giggle. "You'd better wipe the lipstick off. Before your wife sees it."

Roger wiped his hand across his face while Jeanie opened her checkbook and ledger; her new checkbook, with an account made out in her new name. She filled out the total.

With a quick flourish, she signed her name, practicing her new autograph. She tore it off and offered it to the still-red-faced landlord.

He smiled and glanced at it, his smile changing to a frown. "What is this? Who the hell is Maxine Marie?"

"That's me, Roger. Well, that's my new name. Look." She offered her wallet to him, showing her new driver's license. "I made it legal and official earlier this month. And guess what, Rog? You're the first person to get my new signature. It's a whole new me."

Roger squinted at the check. "So I can't call you Jeanie anymore?"

"Oh, well, I suppose it will be all right. but, in a few months, you'll be proud to tell everyone that the world-famous Maxine Marie lives in your apartment building."

"Yeah, right. You ever become world famous, first thing you're doing is leaving this dump." Roger shook his head and pocketed the check. "It had better clear, or I'll be back tomorrow, and I'll be really sore!"

"It'll clear, Rog. Pinky swear." She held up her hand and wiggled her littlest perfectly manicured finger at him. She drew her finger to her lips and kissed it.

Roger left, and she sank into the chair again. Now she was wiped out until the balance of her photo shoot came in. *What horrible luck. Well, five bucks will get me a couple of meals from the diner down the road, so I'll make it, just barely. And, if not, I'll figure out something. I always do.*

1965

Oh, no! I took too many. Something's wrong. Very wrong! The thought drifted to Maxine as if from a great distance. Details of her surroundings phased in and out. She shook her head...or tried. She lacked the strength to accomplish even that simple gesture. She raised her hand to rub her eyes...or tried.

Her vision, her very body, lost distinction from her mind. She could no longer feel the sheet she knew must still cover her torso as she lay helpless. She stared at the phone on the nightstand, above and to the right, the open bottle of pills still atop it, and the *elegant* champagne glass, drained, matching the empty bottle she knew lay on its side on the floor.

I just wanted to sleep. How did this go so wrong?

And this *was* wrong. She drifted, not into a peaceful slumber, but into a numbing, overpowering fading away from existence. A tiny, insignificant spark of panic welled up, screamed for attention, and commanded her numb hands to reach out for the phone. Somehow, she grasped the receiver, but any sense of urgency for her predicament had fled her. She let the phone drop to the bed. In her last effort, she pressed a random button.

"Operator."

The edges of the world had blurred away, and she focused through a fuzzy tunnel. Reality gave way, and she spoke to the tinny angel voice near her ear. *Maybe it's Mom to show me the way?*

But the world slipped away from Maxine Marie for a long, long, long time.

Chapter One

KNOWING HER BOYFRIEND, Daryl Beasley, was expecting her, Loretta Stevens approached his apartment door, gave a quick courtesy knock, and let herself in.

Both had driven away from InfoTech, their mutual place of employment, promptly at 5:00, but Loretta detoured to her apartment to dress down from her work blouse and slacks into something more comfortable for the weekend. Worn jeans, old T-shirt, walking shoes and, for later tonight, underneath her clothes, some new, sexy black underwear.

She walked into the great room. Daryl sat at his usual spot on the long leather couch, oblivious to her presence. On the flat screen TV on the opposite wall, a scene from *Star Trek II* played out.

Undeterred, Loretta walked past the couch and took in the geeky pictures and doo-dads hanging along the wall. Her gaze fell upon the set of memorabilia displayed in a place of honor over the widescreen TV, the curvaceous image of Maxine Marie frozen in a sexy wink. Of all his displays throughout the apartment, the spaceship models, the sci-fi soundtracks, and action figures, only his fixation on the Marvelous Maxine bugged her.

Not much, just a little. She rarely spoke of it. It made no sense to fight about it. And yeah, the classic Maxine movies *were* funny, and she understood the appeal. On the days it really bothered her, she just took him to bed and afterward would think an unspoken, *Top that, Maxine!* in the direction of the shrine of the glamorous sex symbol. *It's so ridiculous to be jealous over a dead woman. I need to get over it.*

She took another step into the room, just enough to slip into his peripheral vision. On the screen, twin yellow phasers of death leapt out from the Reliant and tore an unwanted new gash into the hull of the U.S.S. Enterprise. Screams of pain and blasts of destruction bombarded Loretta from six surround speakers. The carnage cut off in mid-agony as Daryl stabbed the pause button on the remote.

"You're late," Daryl said, not unkindly.

She plopped down next to him. "True. But I'm oh-so-worth the wait." She giggled and slipped into a cheesy imitation of Ricardo Montalban. "Hello, Khirkh! My old...friend!"

Daryl grinned at her. "Stop it. That's not sexy. Well, that's not *supposed* to be sexy. How *do* you do that?"

She placed a hand into her lush red hair and leaned across the couch, batting her eyelashes and puffing her chest out to best draw attention to what Momma called her Georgia homegrown peaches. "Besides, I'm late because I had to change into something special."

Daryl chuckled, looking down at her T-shirt with the black and white image of a tall, skinny man with an egg-shaped head and receding hairline. "Sheldon from *The Big Bang Theory?* You must have me confused with your *other* boyfriend —because that's the last person I want to see later tonight."

She smiled. As Daryl trailed a line of butterfly kisses over her chin and down her neck, a shiver traveled down her body. "Oh, that's not for you. That's for...Oh, that feels good! That's for the *other* nerd girls in the mall. This shirt sends a message that tells them to keep their hands off my man. It's what's *under* the shirt you're gonna love."

His hand drifted up and cupped her breast.

Loretta laughed and batted his hand away. "Later, horndog!"

"Why later?"

"Because we're both hungry and we're shopping for *my* birthday present." She pulled his face close and planted an intense kiss to seal the deal. Separating wetly, she murmured against his cheek. "And if you wait, I promise, you're gonna *love* dessert."

Daryl laughed and stood up. "Okay, let's go." In spite of his feigning disinterest, he had to stop and adjust his pants before walking toward the door.

EVEN ON TUESDAY NIGHT, the congestion of cars surrounded Castleton Square Mall for blocks.

Daryl wrestled the PT Cruiser into a spot some distance from the entrance.

Hand in hand, they crossed the sprawling parking lot toward the glass doors.

Loretta could barely contain herself and started bouncing on her toes beside him.

Not a *skip*, exactly, she was about ten years past her skipping days but, in many ways, she felt like a giddy teenager being taken out and spoiled. "So, man of mine, where are you taking me?" She leaned to one side, placed her head against his shoulder, and batted her eyelashes. "The jewelry store, perhaps?"

Daryl smiled back at her. "Perhaps, as long as you don't want to look at rings."

"Oh, boo on that!"

Daryl stepped forward and held the door open for her, bending at the waist in a half-bow. "Boo, nothing, milady. Did you ever think that I might have my *own* plans to put a ring on your finger when you least expect it?"

A shiver of joy brought her to a stop midway through the door. "Really?" She scanned his expression for a hint.

Daryl kept a poker face. "I simply asked if you'd considered it. If I confirmed anything, then you'd be expecting it, right?"

"Oh, well, then. I should probably still take a peek and point you at certain styles for that one day when I least expect it." *He's gonna pop the question next week!*

"That might be acceptable." Daryl held out his hand, and she gripped it tighter than ever. As she resumed walking, she really did skip. *And I am so gonna say, "yes"!*

Daryl pointed to one of his favorite stop-offs, Famous Frames, a Hollywood souvenir shop specializing in movie posters and autographed memorabilia. "Let's look in here, first."

Loretta nodded. *Maybe the Dave Matthews picture is on sale. That, plus a ring, would make for the best birthday ever.*

"Oh, my God! They have Maxine Marie here!"

Daryl's squeal of fanboy glee from across the room made Loretta cringe. She couldn't control the reflexive eye roll that blurred the framed photo of Dave Matthews she was looking at. Her months-long mantra sprung to her mind, never spoken out loud, but repeated several times daily since they started going out, *Such a geek! But he's* my *geek.*

Out loud, she said, "Maxine Marie at a Hollywood Souvenir Shop? No! Next you'll tell me they have Charlie Chaplin and James Dean, too."

"Yeah, but...I don't know, this is kind of weird."

Loretta gave the autographed Dave Matthews glossy one last longing look before stepping away forever. At 450 bucks, she could see his live show five or six times. *Okay, nosebleed and lawn seats, but still.*

In no hurry, she approached her obsessed boyfriend. On her way, she glanced over several other stacks of overpriced framed goodies on display. *Maxine this, Maxine that.* Last year, Daryl even wanted her to dress up like Maxine for a Halloween party. She supposed he'd meant it as a compliment. Their bust sizes *were* comparable, and Daryl was a lifelong boob fiend, lucky for Loretta. But the last thing she needed was for her co-workers and acquaintances to notice how much she *didn't* look as gorgeous as Maxine Marie! Loretta sighed and reminded herself, once again, that eye candy from the grave could never compare with living, breathing, warm southern comfort!

She wondered, briefly, if she should instead create a Maxine Marie zombie costume, or maybe make herself white and pasty, like a ghost or a vampire, for this year's party. *Now, that had some creative potential. At least then...*Her gaze fell upon the object Daryl clutched between his hands. *What the hell?*

Loretta absorbed the images matted within the gorgeous silver frame, a Maxine Marie publicity photo of the icon in her famous yellow sundress, oozing sex as she arched her back against the support beam of a wooden porch in front of an unidentified backwoods home, one leg hiked behind her and looking every inch like the world's most famous stripper working her pole. Just one of several fallback images her estate printed out as postcards.

Loretta had bought Daryl a stack of them for a random present early in their relationship. This could have been one of them. Loretta also noticed the publicity photo wasn't even signed. Instead, she saw the famous scrawl on a second, much smaller piece of paper matted next to the publicity shot.

Loretta blinked at the paper twice, three times, waiting for her mind to catch up with the message her eyes sent her. The slip of paper in question was the shape and size of a personal check. In fact, it *was* a personal check, made out to the Benson Anders Apartment Complex, in the amount of sixty-five dollars, the letters printed in crooked lines of blue ink across the top line. And in the lower left corner, the double M signature in faded ink.

"No way. Really?" She grabbed the frame, tilting it for a better look around the glare. She examined the faded check, the varying spotted tones of green and blue, eerily similar to a modern counterpart, bank account and routing numbers in their proper places, but the date in the upper right corner read June 19, 1954. Stamped in faded pink, the word "Deposited" and a small date rendered illegible from the ravages of time. Loretta supposed there would be no reason for personal checks to go through a lot of changes in the last half-century, but she still found the whole thing...she struggled to express her disquiet...*tacky.* Really *tacky. It's just not right.*

Out loud, she said, "I don't know. Can you imagine if you ever became famous and, years later, someone framed *your* rent check and sold it to fans at fifteen times what you wrote the check for?"

Daryl shrugged. "I imagine, once you're deceased, and your autograph becomes rarer, anything is fair game."

"I know, but..." Loretta shrugged. "I mean, this check actually *cost* her money when she handed it over. And look at the date. Wasn't that before her first big movie?" Loretta wasn't sure, but she knew Daryl could pinpoint it.

He did not disappoint. "Yeah, *The Hotter, the Better* came out in 1955. That's really when she made it big. Before then—"

"So this was probably a lot of money for her." Loretta knew Daryl would go on for another five minutes with the Maxine Marie movie trivia if she didn't cut him off, even though she'd heard it all plenty of times. "She probably tapped a huge chunk of her checking account at the time, and now, these guys at the store are going to make money off of it."

Daryl's eyes hadn't moved from the framed check since they'd started talking. Finally, his gaze drifted up to her. "You're right."

Loretta released a held breath. "Okay, now put that down, and we'll go find..."

"It's even more rare than I thought. I'm gonna buy it! An early birthday present to myself."

"What?" She fought back a spike of jealousy, not to mention the appalling *waste* of money on her boyfriend's part. Somehow she maintained her composure, even as a double whammy of reactions raced like a cannonball to the top of her head and threatened to blow out through her skull. *We're here for* my *birthday present, not his!*

"I just got my bonus for all that work closing out the

Hendricks project. I was hoping to find something really unique to add to my collection."

"And I thought we were browsing for *me!* Besides, your birthday isn't for another three months." *Mine is next week!*

"Well, I was, but...this is too good to pass up!"

Loretta wanted to scream, but kept her voice to a whisper so only Daryl could hear. "You'd *better* pass that up, or you're going to be passing *me* up, later tonight!"

A VOICE SNAPPED MAXINE AWAKE.

But that's not quite right. Rather, a voice shocked her back into awareness.

She no longer slept. She was no longer even lying horizontal. She stood upright, and she could take in her surroundings with a clear head. She imagined she must have sleepwalked from her home to this brightly lit...very odd store...and awoke while in the midst of sleep-shopping.

She was sandwiched between two young people. A woman's voice called out. "Of course they have Maxine Marie here!"

Oh! I've been recognized, and I must look a wreck! Maxine shook her head to clear it, though actually, her head hadn't been so clear in years.

The man answered with the distracted, enamored tone of voice she knew all too well. "I know, this is just kind of weird." *Oh, no, another admirer. Last thing I need is another jealous girlfriend taking a swing at me.*

"Let's not fight," she said out loud. "I'm happy to sign something, or pose for a picture. Your girlfriend can even take it, so..."

Rather than turn her direction, the young couple closed the distance between them.

Maxine stepped back just in time to avoid bumping into them. They continued to stare with their backs to her at some framed photo.

Well! "Excuse me..." Her voice sounded strangely deep and

canned in her own head, as if she'd covered her own ears before she spoke. "Excuse me?"

The couple continued talking as if they didn't hear her.

Can *they hear me?* "Hey, come on, look at me! You big ugly ass! Stupid bitch! Yeah, I'm talking to you. Turn around!"

But the couple continued to bicker, oblivious to what she said or what she did.

"What the..." Maxine raised her hands to her face, hands she couldn't see!

She reached a finger to her cheek. Upon touching her face, a cold shiver ran through her own body. She looked down at herself, but could see nothing.

I'm invisible. Invisible?! The thought made no sense. *This has to be a dream. Oh, of course it is. The girl who craves attention dreams she's invisible. Oh, Maxine, your shrink will run with this for a month.*

She looked down, confirming she couldn't see the cloth she knew caressed her body as she moved. *At least I'm not naked. My shrink would* never *shut up then. God, I hope I'm wearing something attractive! Though I guess it doesn't matter if I'm invisible.*

And just like that, everything fell into place. She remembered in sharp detail her last moments, lying in bed, struggling to reach for the phone as she slipped into a deep sleep.

A sleep I never awoke from because I died that night. And now, here she stood, a ghost. *Why am I here?*

Once she accepted the truth, her turmoil settled. *The one thing we all fear in life is that moment of death. At least I'm no longer in pain. No more hustle and bustle. No more nagging husbands and panicky assistants. No more awful movie scripts to read through, or cheesecake calendar shoots. No more image to keep up. I can just be myself.*

She drew a deep breath, the easiest, most carefree intake of air she could recall drawing in over twenty years. Then she reflected on the irony of a ghost drawing a breath and she giggled. She also realized that, depending on how long she'd been floating in the bliss of nothingness, it could be long past 1965 by now, maybe even hundreds of years.

Though, looking over the gaudy neon, the fluorescent lights, the small boxy device at the front counter still recognizable as a cash register, she guessed more like decades rather than centuries. She didn't see many signs of advanced technology, no space helmets, no teleporter booths. The man wore what she would have called a polo shirt in her own decade, carpenter shorts and....well, the tennis shoes looked pretty wild, but still recognizable as tennis shoes. The woman wore a T-shirt with the image of a man's face; long, thin, unattractive, almost creepy.

She also recognized the object they quarreled over in a general sense, a plain silver picture frame with a matted set of images. She recognized the cheesy pinup photo from *Farmer's Daughter*, a best-selling poster at the time, and, apparently, still around today. And that idea struck her as just...*elegant!*

The other image, smaller, plain, hard to make out...she stepped closer, right between the couple. She could feel the heat radiating from their bodies, but no actual contact with those bodies. This didn't surprise her as much as she thought it would. She was, after all, dead, and now she could see...

My rent check?

The check I paid to Roger? She still remembered the incident well, even years later, when her growing fame and fortune moved her beyond such concerns as needing to cough up the rent. She could see the total of sixty-five dollars, her address printed in the corner, the spots of sweat as she bent over in front of the fan to write the amount. And then she saw the price tag in the corner, six times the amount filled in for the check itself. *All because I signed it Maxine Marie rather than Jeanne Bracken.*

She'd written that check and sustained herself on chicken soup and half-sandwiches from the diner for the next four days, and now some fat cat store owner was going to collect?

"Weird, what was that?" The quarreling ceased. and the woman raised her shoulders as if to ward off a chill.

Maxine stopped to listen.

"I don't know," the man said, "but I'm buying this, and there's nothing you can do to stop me."

"You buy that picture, and you're taking me straight home afterward!"

"Oh, Loretta, come on, don't be that way!"

"I mean it, Daryl, *straight* home!" By the chastised look on Daryl's face and the stern glare from Loretta, even Maxine understood the subtext. *You tell him! No overnight, no quickie, he can't so much as hold your hand!* Straight *home!*

"Well, I'm sorry you feel that way." With renewed determination, Daryl marched toward the front counter.

"What!" Maxine could not put voice to her shock, but her silent ejaculation matched Loretta's spoken exclamation in perfect synch.

Daryl stomped to the front counter and deposited his framed treasure. Barely containing a huge smirk at his girlfriend, he produced a billfold from his pocket, removed a small card, and handed it toward the man behind the counter.

Maxine guessed the card was some sort of transaction card similar to the Master Charges that were gaining popularity around the time she'd died. "No!" She ran up to the counter and swiped her hand down. Though her hand passed through the card, it flipped out of Daryl's hand and landed on the carpet.

The cashier's face followed the "hopping" card as it jumped into the air and landed on the floor. "Cute trick, mister magician, but I haven't got all day." The cashier folded his hands across his chest.

"But I didn't...sorry!" As Daryl squatted and reached down, Maxine kicked at the card and sent it arcing away from him. "What the?"

Daryl shuffled on the ground after it, slapping his hand down on the card to keep it from jumping further. He found himself on his hands and knees in front of Loretta.

Daryl palmed the card and dropped back onto his haunches, looking up at her. He extended a hand in her direction.

Loretta took a step back and glared down at him with her most devastating glare. "You know what? You're on your own. I'm taking the bus home."

"Loretta, wait!"

Loretta turned and exited the store, blending with the crowd into the main mall walkway.

Daryl struggled to his feet and stared after her.

Maxine, meanwhile, swiped her hands over his arms, but Daryl held his card too tightly for her actions to have any effect. In spite of her efforts, Daryl and the cashier completed the transaction, and, moments later, Daryl left the store, Maxine stomping and fuming alongside him.

Okay, Mister Daryl Whoever-You-Are! You asked for it! You think that *was embarrassing, you haven't seen anything yet!*

Chapter Two

LORETTA STOPPED, blinking back tears as she carefully lowered herself into one of the mall's metal benches, wiping her face and feeling every bit like a high school girl. *Damn him! Seriously? What just happened there?* She felt silly and vulnerable and needy, not to mention *pissed off* that he could make her feel this way, that he had such power over her. *How did I allow that to happen?*

She had to leave, knew it was the right choice as soon as she did it. She had to make a statement. Daryl had to know he was wrong and she would not tolerate such inconsideration. It wasn't even about the birthday present anymore, it was that Daryl had made a choice he knew would hurt her. On purpose. In front of her. *Damn him! That hurt, and he didn't even care!*

God, is this...did we just have our first fight? She thought over the previous months. *First fight? Well, no, not really.* They disagreed all the time, what couple doesn't, but this was their first piss-her-off-and-reduce-her-to-tears confrontation. She never remembered feeling this way. Not ever. *Over anyone.* In all her previous relationships, not that she had a lot, she always kept control, she kept her cool. No man could control her.

But now, this little geek could push her anger buttons and send her over the edge the way no one else had. *And over something so stupid. Damn it.*

She hadn't taken a bus anywhere in months. Fortunately, a quick search on her smartphone told her one was scheduled to leave the mall in five minutes, and that it stopped off at the front entrance to Daryl's apartment complex following a fairly direct route. If she hurried, she could catch it, return to her car parked in front of his apartment, and drive away.

Or she could use her key to his place, let herself in, strip down to her new naughty wear, and wait for him to return; salvage the evening into a quasi-pleasant memory and scold him later over pillow talk. As much as she hated to even admit it, the idea tempted her.

Hell no! That would validate how he treated me. Let him stew overnight.

Minutes later, Loretta took a seat on the bus next to an odd-looking, shriveled old man.

"Hello, lass," he muttered in a thick accent, Maybe Scottish, maybe Irish, Loretta wasn't sure. "No worries now, you're under the protection o' the Transit King."

Loretta glared at him, but his eyes never moved from the window. She sighed. *Crazy people everywhere. Just don't touch me.* She waited out the bumpy bus ride, trying to put her mind elsewhere, to happier times. But all her recent good times had been with Daryl.

IT AMAZED HER, since they started dating over eighteen months ago, how happy Daryl made her. She'd recently moved from InfoTech's Atlanta office to Indianapolis, accepting the department supervisor position in telephone customer service in Indiana for a huge pay raise and more than enough perks to make it worth relocating. Plus, she'd just earned her computer engineering degree, and a move to Indy put her in line the moment a spot opened up in the interface programming department.

Taking the risk had meant a huge break for her, but it also meant leaving everyone she knew.

Normally, she also had a personal no-dating policy in the workplace but, with relocating, she was lonely, and there was something about Daryl.

The interface coding department had a fairly lax dress code, and, being a closet nerd girl herself, she couldn't help but turn her head at his *Star Trek* shirt, his *Star Wars* shirt, his *Aliens* shirt, *Thundercats, Terminator, Doctor Who...*

All she knew was that she wanted to know him better. And then, one day, after roughly two weeks of watching him through one coy peek after another, he approached her table out of the blue.

She still remembered his first words when he took the seat across from her. "Miss, I hope I'm not being too forward, but I've noticed you watching me the past few days. My name is Daryl Beasley, and just in case you're wondering, yes, I am, indeed, one of the lead programmers in the company."

Feeling her face turn bright scarlet, Loretta brought her hands up over her eyes.

Daryl continued, "And if you'll do me the courtesy of accepting my invitation to dinner, I promise to show you an evening you'll never forget." He flashed a charming smile.

Loretta stifled a laugh. *Okay, he knows. I wonder who told him. Or have I really been that obvious?* As her mind raced, she realized a silence had stretched between them.

She lowered her hands, cleared her throat, and smiled back. "Go on, tell me more."

"Well," Daryl placed a hand on the table, almost but not quite touching hers. "The White Castle manager down the road is a personal friend of mine, and I'll bet if I slip him five bucks, he'll reserve the table with the best view."

What a charming goofball! HR policy about public displays of affection be damned, Loretta reached out and placed her hand over his. "Well, Daryl, how can I turn down such an offer?" He'd caught her off guard and had the advantage, and she couldn't allow that to continue. She lowered her voice to give it the perfect husky undertone. "Daryl Beasley, my name is Loretta Stevens. If you can remember that long enough to dial my extension shortly after 5 p.m., I'll give you my cell phone number, and we'll plan this hot excursion to White Castle." She squeezed her eyes shut. "But only if you can tell me the color of my eyes."

She heard Daryl rise, and he gave her hand an affectionate squeeze. "I'll call you at 5:02, and your eyes are a beautiful light blue."

She opened her eyes and beamed at him. "I'll be waiting on that call, Daryl."

MOMMA DIDN'T UNDERSTAND. But she didn't have to. Yeah, Daryl had his moods. He didn't like to leave the house much. He watched sci-fi movies and old movies all the time. And if he was guilty of getting sucked into a Gameboy on his side of the couch, well, she had her own damn Gameboy, and she could clear her own levels as fast as he could. She understood Daryl. Foreplay in the form of several races on *Mario Cart* resulted in sex equal to or greater than foreplay in the form of dinner and a movie, so who was Momma to criticize?

Every week, she'd call her Momma and hear the same complaint. Her last call was no different. "Loretta, I love you, but you should be ashamed of yourself. You're just dating him for his money. *And* you're hoping he can help get you promoted. And he's just sticking around for your Georgia peaches!"

"That's not it, Momma."

"Then what is it? He sounds boring. Loretta, you're thirty-two years old. You're going to be thirty-three in a few days, and you need to start looking for husband material."

Loretta rolled her eyes. "You mean *grandbaby* material, right? And you know what? Maybe I have found husband material."

Loretta let that news hang in the air for a bit before she

continued. "And he's not boring, Momma, he's a geek. But he's *my* geek, and I'm kinda smitten with him. Just be happy for me."

Eighteen months later, Loretta was still kinda smitten with him. Until today.

LORETTA TOOK A DEEP, calming breath. Taking the time to sit and reflect had calmed her. Her pulse no longer pounded in her ears, and she focused her resolve. *I am sure as all hell* not *going to demean myself by waiting for him at his house!*

A thick, accented voice broke in on her train of thought. "Actually, lass, you should reconsider that."

She turned toward the creepy short guy still seated next to her. "Excuse me?'

The little man met her gaze. As best Loretta could recall, this was the first time he'd moved since they'd started their side-by-side trip. The look in his green eyes caused her next word to catch unspoken in her throat.

"Sorry to interrupt, lass. Normally, I just let people mind their business, protect them in their travels. That's all I'm s'posed to do. Get travelers to their destinations safely an' not worry about what happens after. I'm just the Transit King, after all. But you're heading into a big snit o' trouble. As serious a' trouble as I've ever seen."

"Is that right?" The bus slowed, and the old man was seriously starting to freak her out. She rose to her feet.

The little fellow pressed, "Heed my words, lass. Follow yer instincts, not yer pride. Wait for your man tonight. Stay with him. It might help you avoid a kettle full o' trouble later."

"Yeah, look, thanks for the advice, but I'm not really interested."

The bus stopped.

"Sorry you feel that way."

Loretta bee-lined toward the door. She felt the gaze of the old man follow her but thankfully, he stayed in his seat.

Loretta stepped onto the concrete, shaking her head. *No way am I waiting on Daryl to get home with his "prize" and then reward him a second time! I'm heading home right now, and if he misses me, he can call me!*

During the drive back to her apartment, halfway home, the bizarre nature of her exchange with the so-called Transit King finally hit her. He'd offered up specific advice about her problem, but before then, she'd said nothing out loud to the strange old man about Daryl, or what happened tonight. Not one word.

Chapter Three

SEVERAL MINUTES LATER, Daryl stood outside his apartment door, one hand cradling the package against his chest while the other expertly maneuvered the key into the lock. On witnessing this familiar act, Maxine let out a sigh of relief. The tiny, curvy car with its glowing displays from a sci-fi B movie both fascinated and repelled her. She definitely preferred the leather seats from her era over the cup-shaped cloth bastardizations. And there was no room to stretch out! But an apartment, a house key, a lock; not *everything* had changed in this strange new world.

The door opened, and she slipped past. She scanned the unfamiliar surroundings, glancing over the fairly roomy living space (relative to her old apartment—the only one she rented in during her life) from wall to wall, looking for something to break, throw, rattle... *Clearly, I'm here to raise a little hell, and after all, I'm* still *an actress. I can play my part!*

What she saw froze her in place and left her dumbfounded.

On the wall, surrounding the dark rectangular glass screen object she reasoned must be a high-tech version of a television set, hung several framed photos. And she recognized all of them. They were of her at various stages of her career.

In one, she stood before a radio microphone entertaining the troops in Korea; the "clean version" close-up of a bestselling men's magazine photo shoot; and, over there, the publicity shot from *Live and Let Live*, and a photo taken as she sat poolside, when her shoulder strap had broken and she craned her head back toward the camera and offered it a wink.

To see this homage to her, so many photos of poses and candid moments so lovingly arranged into a sort of shrine, overwhelmed her. Sure, she had fans the world over when she was alive. But to see the continued adoration, decades after her death, caused her to swoon.

All the while, Daryl lovingly removed the framed rent check, stepped over to the photos, and rearranged them from nail to nail, creating a space on the wall large enough to accommodate his new acquisition.

Minutes later, they stood, side by side, observing the new configuration of photos.

Eyes still examining the display, Daryl sank into the large leather couch.

Maxine, weightless, dropped and sat next to him.

They both admired the new look.

"Perfect!" exclaimed Daryl into the empty room.

"How...*elegant!*" Maxine said, although he couldn't hear her.

While she contemplated this show of affection for her body of work, (or perhaps just her body) Daryl stepped forward, examining a shelf of what looked like plastic books of some sort. She no longer wished to "haunt" the young man, or cause problems for himself or his loved ones. While the framed rent check still disturbed her, the young man who purchased it did not. *In fact, he's kind of cute.*

While she watched, fascinated, Daryl withdrew some sort of small silver reflective disc, like a toy 45 record, from the plastic box. She recognized the title: *Scratching the Itch*, one of her most popular and critically acclaimed comedy performances.

Moments later, the glass television lit up, the opening credit music belted out from the tower speakers, and the movie began to play in sharp color contrasts and crystal-clear sound. She sat, transfixed, for the next several hours, while Daryl watched a mini Maxine Marie Marathon of *Scratching the Itch*, *The Hotter, the Better*, and *Death at the Falls*, one of her few dramatic films.

Throughout the night, she stole glances at Daryl.

At one point, Daryl had pointed a rectangular doo-dad at the screen, freezing the screen on a perfect close-up of Maxine's face.

As Maxine watched, transfixed at the clarity of her own image, Daryl stepped away into the kitchen.

After a couple of minutes of disquieting popping noises, Daryl returned with a paper bag full of popcorn. *Oh, my! It's like we have our own private screening!*

Daryl settled down next to her, and Maxine leaned forward, whispering in his ear. "I think you're kind of cute, Daryl."

Daryl extended his hand toward the screen, but stopped, as if listening into the air.

She leaned forward and tried again. "This is all so *elegant*, but it's too bad you can't turn off the lights. That would make this even more romantic."

Again, Daryl turned his head and seemed to look directly at her. He grunted, stood, and walked over to some sort of wall panel. To Maxine's shock, the lights in the room dropped to candlelight dimness. Daryl returned to his seat and hit play.

Daryl settled into the show, and Maxine reached her hand out and placed it on his arm. Throughout the movie, she watched him watch her, his face illuminating an odd mixture of adoration and desire. The look triggered a familiar flutter in her stomach.

Maxine curled up next to him, tilting her head against his. "You *can* hear me, can't you?" She giggled in his ear.

Daryl squinted at the screen. "So pretty," he murmured. "She died so young. Such a waste."

EARLY MORNING, midway through *Death in the Falls*, Daryl's eyes shut, and one hand drifted across his own chest. Maxine glanced at the screen to review one of her favorite moments. She watched her image saunter over to the detective and take the cigar from his mouth. Her onscreen image drew the cigar to her lips, inhaled, and blew a billow of smoke into the detective's face.

Maxine leaned over into Daryl's ear, speaking the famous line in synch with the movie. "Tastes a little...stale, detective. Got something else for me to puff on?"

Maxine giggled and looked over at him. "You should have heard how the Fox executive flipped when he viewed the —oh, my!"

While she'd been watching the scene on television, Daryl's hand had drifted down, unsnapped his jeans, and drifted further.

Repelled, Maxine turned away and raised her hand to the side of her face. "Oh, no, Daryl, don't do that. Please, that's..."

She felt herself flush as his breathing increased to a pant.

"Oh, no! Daryl..." But, of course, he couldn't hear her.

She covered her face in her hands, trying to shrivel away, but the reality sank in. *It's not his fault. He's completely alone. Well, he* thinks *he's completely alone. And his girlfriend went home.*

She lowered her face from her hands and turned her head to watch his ministrations. *And this is...well, it's because he likes you.*

Throughout her career, with every photo shoot, with every risqué moment, with every peek-a-boo pose, she'd wanted men to want her. She wanted men to look at her. She longed to be the object of their desire. She was no prude; she'd always understood this. But, until now, she'd never seen the response, and the pun made her giggle, firsthand.

She understood how many men would end up using her photos. She'd accepted that. The idea turned her on, but in a distant, abstract kind of way. She never thought....

She realized that her breaths had increased to a pant along with his. "Daryl!" She watched, boldly now, her eyes following his arm as it vanished beneath the unbuttoned fabric. Now she wanted to see what the fabric hid.

She reached out to grab his wrist, not entirely sure why. Part of her wanted him to stop, another part of her wanted to *help*.

Her hand encircled his upper arm. Her hand registered heat; she could feel his flesh beneath her fingers, and she gripped his wrist.

"Oh! I'm here, baby!" She reached down and caressed her palm against his lap. It was true! She caressed the texture of his jeans, and...*and oh, my!* She could also see the evidence of his arousal. "Daryl. I'm here. I'm...*really* here."

Her fingers danced through his hair, and she leaned forward, her body aching in response to his warmth and solidity. Instinctively, she straddled him, grinding her hips down.

His eyes opened, and Daryl looked up directly at her face. Not through her, as he had all day, but actually directly at her. His mouth dropped open with shock. "What's going on?"

"Shhh. I'm here, Daryl. I don't know how, or why, but I am."

"But you *can't* be. You're dead. This has to be some sort of dream. Wait, get off me!" He reached out, his hands pressing against her shoulders, at first firm, and then changing to an affectionate stroking. "Get off me right...oh, you feel so...amazing!"

"Shhhh, it's okay. It's okay." Through her clothes, she could feel his excitement as she continued to press her hips against him. For her, it was getting beyond okay! Maxine leaned forward, grinding her pelvis down. "Daryl, do you often fantasize about me?"

"I...Well, yeah, but..."

"How does the real thing compare so far?"

"Oh, my God, I can't believe—"

She cut off his answer with a kiss.

He responded a moment later, kissing her back.

All his want and need communicated through a kiss that set her body aflame. *Oh, you are full of surprises, mister!*

She reached one hand up and expertly unfastened the hooks to her dress. It fell around in a pool of ethereal silk. She smiled her best sexy smile at her conquest as she reached a hand down between them, freeing his hips from the jeans and underpants. "Still you want me to stop, big boy?"

"God, no."

She giggled, covering his face with butterfly kisses as she wiggled her hips against him and took him into herself fully. *It's been too long for me, too!* "Tell me how much you want me."

"Yes!"

"Tell me how much you love me."

"I do!"

"Good...Daryl. Soo...good. Soo...soo...*elegant.*" Their mutual cries filled the room as Maxine pulled his face against her breasts. Her full, fleshy, warm breasts.

As he began ministering to her body, the ache of her need forced a deep moan from her. She leaned down and whispered in his ear, commands she knew would bring him over the edge. She leaned back and enjoyed his predicted response.

He groaned.

The heat of her passion building in sync so she joined him in his pleasure. "Soooo ...good, Daryl. So ...good! You're...mine; you're...mine..."

Her climax buckled her body as his final thrust exploded inside her. She held him close, smiling as his body went limp. "You're ...*mine!*"

Chapter Four

Long ago, Daryl had made it a habit to keep a second alarm clock in the main room of his apartment for mornings such as this, when he'd fallen asleep in front of the TV.

Last night, as usual, he'd zoned out on the couch. Unlike other nights, he'd also dreamed the most incredible and realistic erotic dream he could ever remember. Hell, he hadn't even had one of those since late college! *Sex in Dolby Six-Speaker Surround Sound, full 3D realism and feel-tastic flesh tones, and starring a very special guest star from your subconscious, the amazing Maxine Marie.*

Holy shit, what a dream! That was almost worth getting turned down by his real girlfriend. *Almost.* As he stabbed the snooze button and shifted his body to relieve the ache from sleeping on the couch, he resolved to fix the mess he'd made of things with Loretta as soon as he saw her at lunch today. He opened his eyes and slowly stood up. Now all he had to do was...

"Hi, Daryl."

"What the...?"

She lounged across the length of the couch, her lips parted in that famous, devastating smile. Not on his TV screen, but full size, her yellow sundress barely containing her luscious curves. As he drew in a shocked breath, he could *smell* her, an alluring hint of sex and perfume. Then she spoke, "Good morning. I hope you still respect me, Daryl, but if you don't, well..." She shrugged and winked. "That's okay, too."

"But how..." Daryl stopped. Words failed him. Logic failed him. Nothing about this made sense. His brain told his eyes, his nose, his ears, that what they registered before him was bat-shit simply impossible. But as he sat, mute, she rose from the couch and stood before him, in devastating reality, her face now inches from his.

"Daryl?" She emitted that incredibly cute giggle. "I know, it's...a bit intense, I imagine."

"No!" He stepped back, hands folded across his chest, self-conscious of his rumpled look. "No. No *fucking* way. Who the hell are you?"

"I'm Maxine, Daryl. I know, it sounds fantastic, impossible, fantastically impossible, whatever you want to call it, but——"

"Bullshit, you're Maxine! Is this some sort of sick joke by Loretta?" He realized as soon as he said it how impossible that was. Sexually, Loretta could be pretty adventurous at times, but her perch just didn't swing this direction. Loretta would never instigate, let alone condone, a scenario where he ended up getting laid by a Maxine Marie lookalike.

And what a lookalike! "Jesus, you look just like her!"

"No, Daryl, I'm really me. I mean, I'm really Maxine. It's confusing, but——"

"Maxine Marie died over fifty years ago! There's no *fucking* way you are Maxine Marie!"

"Daryl!" Her eyes had widened at his expletive, responding like someone truly not used to hearing people curse casually. "I know, this is really weird. It's really, really weird. But look." As he watched, her body literally dimmed, then turned ethereal, and she slowly vanished.

A giggle rode upon the air, and she "phased in" again, apparently having taken three steps to her left.

"No way!"

"Yes, it's true, Daryl. I've been with you since you purchased this..." she waved her hand at the wall, specifically at the rent check. "This check thing. But I couldn't talk to you. You couldn't see me. Until last night. Then, somehow, there I was. And, overnight, I've been experimenting. I'm getting pretty good. I can control it. Look." She reached out and gripped his hand.

He wanted to pull away, though her alluring warmth caused an arousing stir. Then her hand was no longer there, and his hand passed through her. He could see the outline of his couch through her body.

Maxine solidified and gripped his hand again. "See? I'm getting better. Stronger. I don't want to scare you, but...more powerful. Like..."

"A ghost," Daryl finished.

Maxine...he had to accept her identity...drew in a breath and released it in a sigh of frustration. "A ghost." She shrugged and grinned. "Boo."

"You're not very scary for a ghost."

"Yeah, well, I'm kind of new to this haunting thing."

Daryl sank back down into the couch and covered his face in his hands. His head spun, the edges of reality blurring. His brain still screamed in the back of his head, *Bullshit! Foul! No way is this happening!* And yet, he had to find some way to accept it.

As she sat down next to him, he sensed, rather than saw, the reality of her. The warmth of her arms around him spoke of her solidity. She felt *so* good, *so* real, here in the room. And her voice, "It's okay, Daryl. I'm a little freaked out about it, too."

"But how can you be here now? Why me? You have millions of fans all over the world."

"I do?" She sounded genuinely shocked to hear this news.

"And you...you don't haunt people. Look, I'm a big fan. I know all the stories and the rumors. If you haunted fans, I would have heard about it."

"Well, I don't. That is, well, you're the first. By the way, what year is it?"

"2012."

"Oh, ...my, so, I've lost almost fifty years...wow!"

"Really? So the last thing you remember is..." he hesitated.

Maxine finished. "I tried to call the hospital after I took too many pills." She shrugged. "I couldn't sleep, and I guess I overdid it."

"So it wasn't suicide?"

"Oh, goodness, no!"

"And no one tried to kill you?"

"Huh?" She shook her head and scoffed. "Don't be ridiculous. Why would you think that?"

"It's one of the wilder conspiracy theories. My favorite is that gangsters killed you with a deadly enema."

Her uneasy giggle brought a smile to his face. "How absurd. No one killed me, and I didn't even mean to commit suicide. I just made a mistake. I couldn't sleep, and I did something that wasn't very smart, but it had worked before. I take a tranquilizer with every sip of champagne until I fall asleep. Went through the entire bottle of champagne, and I don't know how many pills." Her hand squeezed his.

He looked up into her doll-like, pale face.

"I remember ...being so scared when I couldn't move. I hate being alone. I *hate* it. And I couldn't move, and I couldn't call anyone, and I was turning numb and I knew...I *knew* I was going to die...and I'd be all alone when it happened."

Tears trickled down her face. He reached out and brushed the wetness with a knuckle. "I'm sorry."

Maxine smiled. "What for? I finally fell asleep. And I stayed asleep for a long, long time. Do something stupid and become a legend. Who knew?" She sniffled, her face distorted in sadness. "Do something so stupid that even the rent check you wrote to keep from ending up in the street becomes a valuable collector's item to the vultures."

"Rent check?" Daryl glanced at the framed image and back at her. "You think that's what this is about?"

"I don't know. I just know that the first thing I remember...as a ghost, I mean...was standing between you two while you fought over whether you'd buy the check."

Daryl considered. "I suppose that makes sense. How do you feel about it?"

Maxine folded her arms across her chest and glared. "Gee, I don't know, Mister. How would *you* feel about seeing your personal check framed and for sale at a souvenir shop?"

"Well...I suppose I'd be pretty pissed about it."

Maxine's eyebrows furrowed. "Yes, indeed, though I've never heard the word 'piss' used exactly that way. In any case, I was angry enough to knock your Master Charge from your hand."

"That was you?"

She nodded.

"Wow." He stood and retreated to his bedroom. He returned moments later, pulling a light blue polo T-shirt over his head.

Her eyes reflected concern. "Where are you going?"

"Work. I have to go."

"Can't you stay home today?"

Don't I wish! "I'm sorry. I have to work. I'm a computer engineer. I can't just...not show up. We're in the middle of something big, and they need me. It would be irresponsible to not be there. That's not how I roll."

"I don't know what a computer engineer does, but you have to roll something?"

"Never mind. I mean, I'm not going to ignore my responsibilities."

"Well, okay, but I'm going with you."

Daryl stepped toward the door, running a comb through his tangled hair. "I don't think that's a good idea."

"I'll be good, Daryl. I'll stay invisible and won't touch a thing."

The potential for trouble boggled his mind. "Sorry, Maxine, that's still a terrible idea." He opened the door and stepped into the bright August sunlight, the heat already oppressive at 7:00 a.m. In spite of his words, he waited.

"You'll barely know I'm there, I'll be as quiet as...." Ironically,

Maxine emitted a squeak. She bounced back from the door entrance as if hitting some sort of vertical energy "trampoline" that sent her sprawling backward, where she landed on her ass with an indignant yelp.

Daryl felt bad for her, but mostly relieved for himself. He hadn't talked to Loretta yet, and he had no idea where to start. The last thing he needed was a possessive ghost eavesdropping in on the conversation.

"Maxine. I *will* be back."

"Daryl, wait, don't go!"

"I have to work, Maxine. Just stay where you are. Make yourself at home. Help yourself to any food if you need it."

"I'm not the least bit hungry...for food!"

Daryl considered, the implication of her come-on not lost on him. But...*No, bad idea.* "Well, I'm sorry, but that's going to have to wait, too."

"You can just take the picture with you into work! Wait, Daryl!"

She reached out and gripped his arm. A spark of some sort of energy made itself visible at the door entrance. Given all the impossible events of the last few hours, he accepted the energy barrier with nonchalance. He sensed that if he pulled hard enough, he could separate himself and shut the door in spite of her protests. But he didn't want to leave with her mad.

"I'll be back, promptly at 5:30. Look, I have an entire shelf in my bedroom devoted to biographies of you. Check them out. Tonight, I'll show you how to operate the TV, but I don't have time now."

"Daryl Beasley, you get back here this instant! I mean it!"

"Maxine, please." He had two women mad at him, something unique in Daryl's experience, and he didn't know how to handle it. "I'm sorry, I have to go!"

He pulled his arm free and shut the door in her face.

HE DROPPED down into the seat of his car and just sat. Boggled, dazed, overwhelmed, none of the standard clichés quite covered the turmoil that overwhelmed him.

Time ticked away, and as he racked up his first-ever tardy on his perfect work attendance, he let the silence percolate around him. He kept waiting for his brain to "get it," to accept what had happened, so he could go forward.

But it didn't.

Last night, I slept with Maxine Marie. The real Maxine Marie.

Nothing. The thought equated to saying he'd just taken a ride in Santa Claus' sleigh, or been picked up by the Doctor and they'd taken the TARDIS for a spin.

He tried taking a mental step back. The real Maxine Marie is lounging in my apartment. Okay, a damn beautiful woman who looks like Maxine Marie is in your apartment and can't wait for you to return home.

He'd just talked to that beautiful woman, so he knew that much was true. And his body certainly responded to the memory of speaking with her.

Last night, I cheated on my girlfriend with Maxine Marie. Though, technically, she just appeared nearly naked and already straddling me by the time I knew what was even happening. How could I refuse?

Yeah, that would go over well. The fact that it happened to be the truth didn't really matter.

The thought made his stomach lurch. *I have a beautiful woman in my apartment. I have Maxine Marie. I have her all to myself.*

Last night I slept with Maxine Marie. And she made it clear she wants to sleep with me again.

A sharp pain stabbed at his stomach. And no wonder. The guilt of what happened had probably settled in on him. He didn't deal well with guilt. *How did I get stuck in this situation? What in the hell am I going to tell Loretta?*

You don't have to tell her anything. The thought came to him as if from someone else, but he knew it was his mind taking up both sides of the issue.

Yes, I do. Of course, I do. I love her. She loves me. She deserves to know.

So what are you going to tell her, exactly?

He stuck the key in the ignition and started the engine. The pain poked at him again, causing him to wince.

I'll think of something and make it right. And then I'll come home and...sort all this out with Maxine, too. Somehow.

THOUGH LORETTA KNEW Daryl could never really stay mad at her, she breathed a sigh of relief when she saw him already at "their" table like last night had never happened. She sat across from him and spoke the line she'd been rehearsing in her head all morning. "I'm still mad at you, but if you buy me dinner, I've decided that will make up for it."

Daryl glanced up from his microwave lasagna; his face didn't crack so much as a smile.

Undeterred, Loretta leaned forward, knowing her scoop-neck sweater offered him an exclusive and tempting peek at her ample cleavage. "Pay attention, young man. I said, buy me dinner and you're forgiven. And, if I do say so myself, that's mighty generous of me. So you'd better *jump* at this one-time exclusive offer." She knew Daryl's sex-obsessed mind would not miss her emphasis on the word "jump."

When he looked up again, she tried not to cringe. At first, she thought old man Snopes must have been running him ragged with demands for new code. But now, she could see he hadn't shaved, and, as they remained in close proximity, her nose twitched, confirming that he hadn't bathed, either. And something else, a randy odor, like...*no way. He just whacked off to his porn or something.* The thought made her smile. *He digs me. And I* did *leave him with a terrible case of blue balls, after all.* She also saw the dark circles under his eyes. *Poor Daryl. Our fight must have kept him up all night, and he must have woken up late.*

She pressed her advantage. "Look, I'm sorry. I didn't like walking out on you, but you can't treat me like that and not expect consequences."

"Huh? What consequences?"

Loretta quietly fumed at his response, but attributed it to fatigue. "All right, look. We'll have a late dinner, after you go home, shave, and shower. Maybe I'll even join you if you're really nice to me between now and five. I should probably have my head examined for wanting to stay with an obsessed geek, but you're *my* obsessed geek, and I'm kind of smitten with you. So rather than dwell on what happened—"

"I can't Loretta. It's over."

"What?" Her head spun at this unexpected shift in the conversation. She couldn't have been more surprised if Daryl had declared a secret love for guys and his intent to have a sex change. She thought, ...no, she *knew*...her light-hearted, take-charge girlfriend act would bring him around. But, in spite of her bravado, she really didn't want to lose him. "Daryl, what are you saying?"

"I want to break up, Loretta. I'm sorry." Without another word, Daryl rose to his feet and dropped his paper napkin over his untouched microwave meal. "I don't feel very good. I'm taking the rest of the day off."

She could only sit, words stuck in her throat, and watch Daryl walk out of the room. For the next several minutes, a mix of emotions ground in the pit of her stomach and anchored her to her seat.

Chapter Five

Daryl stood outside the door, pressing his ear against the wood. He closed his eyes against a sudden wave of nausea.

He heard his stomach growl. When had he last eaten? He'd skipped breakfast, only nibbled on lunch. Usually he bought a breakfast pastry or something, even if it was just packaged preservative-filled crap from the vending machine, but this morning, he'd forgotten. So nothing but coffee since the popcorn last night. He needed to eat as soon as possible.

He hated walking away from Loretta. He hated playing the sick card. In his five years as InfoTech's lead interface programmer, he almost never called off to go home sick, so his boss took him at his word. *Thank God for small favors!* For now, the ghost of Maxine Marie, alone in his apartment, mad as hell at him, filled his thoughts.

He didn't hear anything on the other side of the door, but he just *knew* the apartment was trashed. In her fury, Maxine had probably sent all his collectibles spinning into a whirlwind like that crazy scene from *Poltergeist*. His *Star Trek* Starship *Enterprise-D* model kit, his TARDIS Police Box, his Jerry Goldsmith Complete *Planet of the Apes* soundtrack. Any and all of it could be trashed in a moment of anger. Hell, she probably even trashed his framed Maxine Marie U.S. Postage Stamps and wall clock, just to get back at him.

He braced himself for the worst, turned the knob, and pushed through in one motion. Ready, he hoped, for whatever he may see on the other side.

Anything, that is, but what he *did* see.

The main room picked up. Spotless. His old, dirty clothes, strung here and there on the floor, chair, the couch, all gone. He wondered if she washed them. Stacks of gaming and girlie magazines, gone. Hopefully, that meant the mags were picked up and stored somewhere and not truly gone. The rug showed the distinct mini-wheel trails of someone having run a vacuum, and lacked the usual debris of lint and specks he'd grown accustomed to in his life of eternal bachelorhood.

A book hovered in the air several inches above his couch. Odd, how quickly his mind now dismissed such a sight as "normal." Presumably, the book was held open by unseen hands, positioned exactly as if an invisible sexpot were reading and reclining. He craned his neck to take in the volume. She'd picked *The Icon, an Unauthorized Biography of Maxine Marie.* That particular book recapped the trashier rumors circulating about Maxine, such as the leading men (and in some cases leading women) she'd slept with during the entire arc of her career, including dozens of stories of unsubstantiated and sensational gossip.

He heard Maxine's disembodied voice from the direction of the couch. "You're home early! I'm so glad."

Daryl nodded. "Fun reading?"

"My goodness, Daryl. If I really slept with every person this book claims I did, I'd have had no time to ever make a picture! At least, not the sort of picture I'd want anyone to see!" A body-less giggle filled the room.

He sat in his leather recliner and rotated it halfway around, centering the couch in his vision. "That's probably not the best book to start with."

"I can't believe how much they quote Bart Perry." She

released a disembodied sigh into the room. "Sure, he was a great baseball player, and he didn't confine his home runs to the stadium, either, if you know what I mean. But I couldn't so much as sign for a telegram without him accosting the delivery boy and demanding to know if I'd slept with him!"

Daryl didn't really want to hear anything more about the sexual prowess of Maxine's baseball-legend ex-husband. "Could you...uh...could I see you?"

"Huh? Oh, my! I didn't even realize."

A moment later, Maxine's physical body phased to full visibility. She wore the same yellow sundress from last night, looking a bit rumpled, but still serviceable. She flashed him a grin that melted his heart.

He drew a deep breath. "Wow, you're so beautiful. I just can't believe you're here. That you're *really* here."

"You're sweet, Daryl. Can I get a kiss?"

She didn't have to ask twice. Without another word, he rose from the chair and leaned over her. The kiss was electric, full of wetness and hunger and need. *Is that just me wanting her? Or could it possibly be—*

"I missed you, Daryl. I'm glad you're home early."

"Wow!"

"What?"

"I mean, me, too."

"You're so sweet when you're bashful." She placed her palm against his cheek. "You're going to have to get used to me. This is still your home, you know; I'm just haunting it."

Her touch made him swoon. He started to put his head down, hesitated, then realized if she didn't want him to presume familiarity, she probably would not have introduced herself by fucking his brains out.

So he lay his head down on her stomach and enjoyed the sight of looking between the mounds of the world's most famous cleavage. "But you don't know, Maxine. It's like, if Charlie Chaplin or Rudolph Valentino were a ghost in your era and haunted your house. But it's not. It's bigger than that. You've become *the* Hollywood sex icon of '60s Hollywood."

"Wow, really?" Her hand drifted down and scratched his head.

He closed his eyes, drinking in every moment like sensual cocaine, his head spinning from the affection.

"You can't think of anyone else you'd rather have haunt you? What about Grace Kelly?" She giggled.

Her question surprised Daryl, "According to a lot of my biographies, you two really hated each other. Is there any truth to that?"

"Absolutely not! Well...my agent put my name in when he heard about *To Catch a Thief*." Her giggle lit up her face. "He was *so* sure I would get it. And who wouldn't want it? Alfred Hitchcock, Cary Grant, it just doesn't get *any* yummier than that!" She smiled, and her eyes took on a faraway look. "But, no, I'd just landed my first major role, and the movie hadn't even come out yet. I knew I had no chance."

"So no anger over losing the part to her?"

Maxine shook her head, the blonde waves radiating a warm glow. "No. I kinda liked her, myself. She was so *elegant*, Truth is, she was a lot more talented than I was. It always seemed like no one would take me seriously. But you didn't answer my question, mister. You think she's quite a dish, don't you?" Her eyes reflected amusement as she teased him.

"Princess Grace was awesome in her own ways. But, ultimately, she doesn't hold a candle to you." He reached out, gripped her hand, and brought it to his lips.

"Ah, that's sweet. I like you, Daryl."

The comment hung between them as he drank in her words.

Her eyes drifted, and he wondered what quaint memory had captured her, what memory from an entirely different time in a world he'd only read about.

Finally, her eyes refocused, and her gaze held his once again. "Hey, did you know I met Prince Ranier? He showed up to a couple of movie premieres when I was filming out in England. He never hit on me, though. A perfect gentleman, darn the luck." She let out a playful squeal, and Daryl felt her stomach tense as she stretched across the couch. She looked like a cat protecting her territory. "Grace Kelly's probably an old lady now."

"She died in a car accident in 1981."

Her face distorted, like someone had pinched her. "Oh, that's...that's terrible. How sad."

Silence hung between them. Daryl kissed the back of her hand. "Don't be sad. She's probably haunting some young stud, too."

Maxine laughed and sighed. Her hand stroked, feather-like, over his cheek and returned to scratching his head.

"What about Jean Harlow?"

"A good-looking woman, to be sure. But, no. Your movies were funnier." He leaned in for another kiss.

Her lips broke their kiss and parted in a smile. "Ingrid Bergman?" she murmured against his cheek.

Daryl pretended to consider. "Definitely a hot accent."

Maxine pulled back and met his gaze, her look stern but teasing. "She was damn fine-looking, too. Come on, admit it, Daryl!"

Daryl laughed and covered her mouth with his. They parted wetly. "I still like you better."

"Oh! Tell me why, Daryl."

His hand drifted to her breast. As his fingers danced over the thin fabric, her nipple hardened. "Because, silly, you were in full color..." His lips traced a path down her neck. "VistaVision..." He planted a light kiss, and her body squirmed in response. "...and stereo sound."

"Oh...Do you want me?"

"Do you have to ask?"

She trailed her hand down between their bodies. "Yes. I want to hear you say it."

"Yes."

"Do you love me?"

"Yes!"

She leaned forward, whispering. "Are you mine?"

"Yes."

Her smile widened, and her gaze sharpened to a sexy-wicked gleam that penetrated to his soul.

With sudden force, her hands clasped the front of his shirt. She shoved him off her, pushing him on his back and onto the floor.

Daryl landed on the carpet, stunned. Before he could react, Maxine pounced on top of him, her mouth over his, pressing hungrily. "Love me, Daryl. Just love me. Be mine!"

"OH, DARYL! LET'S GO OUTSIDE!" Maxine's begging voice roused Daryl from a deep sleep. A gust of cold air brushed across his legs. Still only half awake, he thought, *Huh. Ghosts really do cause cold spots.*

He opened his eyes to find himself sprawled on the floor, shivering, his pants still down around his ankles from when Maxine had attacked him. Across the room, Maxine stood at the entrance of the back-glass patio door. He peered out into the darkness, seeing moonlight gleam off the retention pond in back. *What the—?*

He stood, pulling his pants up and hoping to God no one across the water had looked his direction. Just as he adjusted his pants up and across his waist, a wave of dizziness caused his legs to give out. He fell back and sank into the couch. *I gotta eat!* "Shut the door, Maxine!"

"But I want to go outside!" she whined. To prove her point, she extended her hand, palm out, toward the door opening. A current of static energy flickered across the entrance. She pressed harder, the current increasing. Sparks of static shot in all directions. She stopped and looked back at him, a pout disfiguring her gorgeous face. "See? And I can't carry the picture myself. I tried!"

With a final squeal of anger, she threw her hands up in the air and began pacing the great room. "I guess it's forbidden for us ghosts to interact with certain things, like the item that called us here in the first place, not that we would know that. Us ghosts didn't get a free handbook when we're summoned." She stopped pacing and looked at Daryl. "Did you get a handbook?"

"Uh...no."

"There, you see? She held her arms out and called out to the ceiling. "So how are we supposed to know the ghost rules? Now, Daryl, pay attention. I can't move this frame or this picture, which means it's up to you to be my hero. I know, it's a tough task, but it's 'the rules,' and we're both stuck with them." She put her hands on her hips and released an exaggerated sigh.

Daryl stifled a chuckle. *She's acting, turning on the charm to make me do what she wants. And dammit, it's working.*

She motioned to the spot on the floor where he'd been sleeping moments earlier. "And then, I couldn't wake you up, so..." she trailed off and motioned to the open door.

"Okay, give me a second." He took a few shaky steps toward the kitchen, wondering if he still had a granola bar or something to tide him over. "I need to eat something first."

"Oh, shit, Daryl! You can come right back afterward. Just take the picture frame outside first. The pond looks *delicious*!"

"But I haven't eaten anything all day."

"Oh, pooh! I haven't been outside in over fifty years. That means if I breathe in forty-nine-year-old air, it's still fresh to me! Trust me, mister, it's been a *long* time. But that's okay; you just go on and have your silly sandwich first."

Christ. He opened a cabinet and grabbed the last granola bar in the box. He looked across the room to see Maxine staring at him, her upper lip extended in an exaggerated pout, her eyes watching him hopefully. "Okay, I guess this will do. I'll get something more in a little bit."

The chastising tone vanished. "Thank you, Daryl; you are making me *so* happy!"

He shuffled over to the wall and took the framed check down off its hook. He stepped toward the patio door opening and stopped as another bout of dizziness overtook him. He reached out with one hand and gripped the patio door handle, waiting for the moment to pass. Still walking on rubbery legs, he worked his way out onto the porch, holding the picture under his arm.

Maxine ran out the door. Letting out a squeal, she darted past Daryl and across the porch, slowing just enough to take the two wooden steps to ground level.

Daryl shuffled after her, bemused, watching Maxine's sundress literally fall from her body into a cloth pile on the shore of the pond.

He heard two or three splashes and a playful scream. She dropped down into the water. He wondered if anyone was watching after dark. If so, they were in for the show of their lives. *Ghost of Maxine Marie seen skinny-dipping in Walden Apartments Pond! Film at eleven—uncensored video on YouTube!*

Apparently, his neighbors weren't looking outside, or they were watching in secret. A quick glance at his watch answered why. He's slept through the evening; it was now 12:30 a.m. *I don't feel like I've slept that long. Hell, I could use another twelve hours, easy.*

He gripped the wooden railing and held on for dear life, hobbling along...*one step, two steps, grass...*to ground level.

He heard more splashing and giggles. "Come on, let's have some fun, you old fuddy-duddy!" She splashed water at him.

Daryl held his arms up. Ice-cold water sprayed his arms and face. "Stop it, Maxine!"

"Oh, pooh! Are you coming in, or not?"

He considered, but, even while he thought about it, his legs gave way, and he dropped to the ground, landing on his ass with an ungraceful thump. Instead, he just took in the sight of her bobbing up over the water, her eyes sparkling in the moonlight, her hair slicked back against her head, the water dancing along her cleavage. Her lips curled up in a sexy-wicked smile. "Come on in, Daryl. The water's fine, and so am I!"

Now damp, his body shivered as he watched her. He wanted to go to her. He liked to see her happy, having fun, but he couldn't join her. "I can't. I'm too tired. I just need to rest for a while. It's okay, you can..."

But she'd already ducked underwater.

He'd been dismissed.

With a weary sigh, he let himself fall back on the grass. He lay there, cradling the picture frame, listening to her playful frolicking, until he drifted off into a deep, dreamless sleep.

At first, she enjoyed the simple pleasure of immersing her body. How long had it been since she'd last had a chance to swim? *Well, much longer than I can even recall, that's for sure!*

To swim, to float, to close her eyes and thrill to the current her body created as it broke through the water. The bubbles! They tickled and tingled all over! While she lived, she loved swimming. To drop away from the world, to block everything out. To float and just *be.*

Until she ran out of air, when the need of her body would battle with her desire to stay under, stay down, to stay away from everything...forever. Then her need for oxygen would *force* her to the surface, to rise and breathe.

Which...should have happened some time ago.

She opened her eyes in the depths of the blackness. Fish and water lilies brushed past. Her eyes stung, just a bit, but not how she remembered they should. And...she could breathe. She floated in the space between the upper surface and the mossy floor.

I could stay here all night! I could stay here for days! She knew she had no need to eat or drink. And there were other changes. Vibrant, intoxicating changes she couldn't begin to understand.

If only Daryl weren't such a fuddy-duddy! I want to play; I want to swim! I want to make love on the shore. I want to run through the grass and feel the moss tickle my toes. And there he is. Asleep!

Her body awakened. Her senses sharpened. The world snapped into focus. What she saw, what she heard, what she tasted, what she touched, had broadened past the "normal" of living reality, and expanded, into some *beyond.*

She reached out, sliced a hand through the water. She sensed the bubbles, the fish, and the life all around her. Sensations of bubbles caressed her body. Slow, gentle, calming, she wished the current would flow in a more powerful wave.

And at the speed of thought, it did.

At her command, the waves built up to a more insistent throb.

Oh, my goodness! Did I *do that?*

The current stroked her, causing answering tingles of sensation through her hair, over her face, her entire body. The current bent to her whim. *I* did *do that!*

She willed the current to reverse itself, to tap and knead against a knot in her shoulder, to caress her thighs, to stroke her like a lover, to bring her to orgasm right there in the midst of the lake.

Her cries of pleasure washed away in the current.

This was so *beyond* elegant! So beyond what she'd ever known in life. And she wanted more!

She drifted toward the surface, not by the force of her kicks, and not through swimming. She'd grown beyond that!

She broke the surface of the water, arching up like a supernatural sea creature, but she didn't come back down to the water. Gravity had no effect on her now. She kept going, up, and up, until she hovered over the water, her arms extended to either side, droplets pouring down into the pond.

A shiver of pleasure and power coursed through her, the tremors forcing a moan from her. She clasped her hands into fists against the onrush of energy. Water sprayed from her body, erupting in all directions, leaping from her skin like a current, to land several yards in every direction around her. Her hair danced around her head as the water shook itself free.

A gust of air held her body suspended. At her thought, the air lowered her body back down toward the surface of the water. She dropped and extended one foot. She "dipped" the toe into the water, imagining herself dangling like a giant tea bag on a string. The rush of cold made her giggle.

She stared into the pond, sensing the strength, the growing power. Focusing her energy, channeling it, she could maybe...

A blast of pond water exploded beneath her, a spraying a jet of foam that covered and coaxed, made her shiver. She motioned to her left, and a second blast burst and poured its liquid life over her. To her right, left, front, back, all at once in succession, as explosive sprays of liquid poured over her in a white noise current, causing a rush of pleasure that made her come again.

Spent for the moment, she looked down on the crumpled, slumbering form on the land some distance away. *Daryl missed it. Doesn't that just figure?*

With a simple thought and motion, I could send a wave onto the shore and make *him join me! He'd be pulled into my currents before he knew it, completely at my mercy.*

She raised her hand to command the wave to pour down upon him. *Here it comes, Mister Fuddy Duddy! You better watch out. You don't want to play? Too bad. I'm going to* make *you play.*

But a realization held her back. *This all started with Daryl. What's happening with me has something to do with him. I still need him. I have to hold on to him. I have to keep him, make him mine, forever. Because whatever's happening to me...I like it!*

Chapter Six

It took three hours before Loretta Griffin found a break in her calls.

Technically, that wasn't quite true. As supervisor of the help desk, she could have disconnected from the incoming stream of calls at will. But it wouldn't be fair to her team, to leave them a person short when the average hold time was over ten minutes. It was not how she rolled. But ever since InfoTech introduced the new MP3 upgrade, customers' units had been bugging for days, and the helpdesk was lit up with complaints.

Small blessing. Daryl hadn't programmed that particular problem, or she'd have even more to give him hell about.

When she'd first clocked in, she dialed his work extension, and then called his cell phone. No response. She told herself she would not, not (hell no she would *not!*) go out of her way two floors up to drop in on his department. Such actions communicated desperation. She was *not* desperate.

So now, a half hour prior to lunch break, she disconnected her headphones from the active calls and stomped toward the elevator. *Dammit! He's gonna give me the silent treatment? He's gonna make me go talk to him?*

She stepped into the elevator and stabbed the button for the fourth floor. The doors shut, and she yelled at the ceiling. "Fine, Daryl Beasley! I'm desperate! But this is *so* going to cost you! I will *not* let you break up with me over some goddamn dumb *dead* blonde actress, even if she *is* Maxine Ma—" The doors slid open, and she stopped mid-rant as she found herself face to face with Vice President Rooney Smith. She offered him an abashed grin and a nod. As he stepped past, Smith glared at her. Smith glared at everyone, so that didn't necessarily mean anything. "Hello, Mister Smith."

"Good to see you," he mumbled, his standard response whenever he saw her. Loretta suspected his response was code for, "I don't know you, I don't know your name, but I know you've worked here more than three months. Your brown-nosing is duly noted."

Loretta stomped down the hall, past a break station, and turned the corner, closing in on the mini-cubicle city that made up the interface programming department. Twin rows of cubicles extended along two walls, and, against the third, a closed executive office door next to the open door of an unlit, empty conference room. And in the middle, the executive receptionist's desk formed the hub to the cluster. Loretta looked away, but it was already too late.

The executive secretary called out. "Hi, Loretta!"

Flushing, Loretta waved at the blond woman at the desk. "Hi, Monica."

The secretary's eyes looked over the lenses of her glasses and followed as Loretta approached Daryl's cubicle. "Uh, wait, he's not..."

Loretta turned the corner and stopped at the gap that served as Daryl's "door," where the cube wall met the real one. "Knock, knock busybody, just thought I'd see how..." She stopped in mid-sentence, realizing she stared at an empty office chair pushed against a cleared desk that clearly had not been occupied today. She blew out a frustrated breath, her eyes catching the familiar image of a Maxine Marie publicity poster pinned to the far wall. *God, shoot me now!*

She turned to see several males leaning halfway out of their cubes, all watching her with looks ranging from shock to amusement.

Flushing so hard her ears hurt, Loretta offered a wave to her gawking audience and stepped toward the receptionist's desk. "Hello, everyone. Sorry to bother you."

She closed the distance to the reception desk and leaned forward, offering the smirking woman her most intimidating glare and speaking in a near-whisper. "You...*might*...have...stopped...me!"

Clearly not intimidated, Monica returned an amused smile. "I tried, honey."

"You...*might*...have...tried...*harder*!"

"And miss you get all red in the face?" In spite of her ribbing, Monica offered a sympathetic shake of her head.

Loretta swallowed, bracing herself as she asked the question foremost on her mind. "So, where is he?"

Monica shrugged, her tone now serious. "Actually, I thought you were coming up to tell me. We haven't heard from him all morning." Monica indicated the closed office door with a toss of her head. "The old man is pretty pissed, too. We're in the middle of crunch time. Daryl picked a hell of a time to go off the radar."

"He didn't call in?"

"Not a word. The only reason I'm not filling out his pink slip with H R is that this just isn't like him. Frankly, I'm a bit worried. Like I said, I'd hoped you knew something."

Loretta's breath caught in her throat at the news. "I'm sorry, I don't know where he is."

"But you *do* know something," Monica prodded.

Before she could stop herself, Loretta blurted, "I know he broke up with me yesterday for no good reason."

"Oh, honey!" To her credit, Monica also kept her voice low. "That man *is* sick if he can't recognize what a good thing he has with you."

"Well...thanks."

Loretta started to move away, but Monica followed up. "So what was his official no-good reason?"

Loretta considered. She'd lost a lot of sleep over their problems, and before she knew it, the words tumbled out of her mouth. "We got into a fight when he bought a Maxine Marie photo instead of my birthday present."

"Well," Monica shrugged, "I'll grant you, that's a shitty thing to do, but you just gotta work past that."

Loretta shook her head. "No, you don't understand. Yesterday I told him I was over it, but *he* still broke up with *me*."

"Oh." An awkward pause hung between them. Loretta realized she'd been staring at the carpet and risked a look up.

The receptionist looked thoughtful. "Well, that's...very odd." Monica drummed her fingernails on the paper surface of her desktop calendar. "This is just a hunch, honey. But whatever else is going on, I don't think he broke up with you over the picture of some dead movie star hussy. And that is *certainly* not why he is ducking out from work."

Loretta swallowed. "So you think..."

"That whatever's keeping him in the house is very much alive, warm," she dropped her voice to nearly inaudible, "and fucking your boyfriend." Monica punctuated her conclusion with a sharp nod.

"Thanks."

"Don't mention it. I just hope he's not off on a cruise with the other woman somewhere."

Loretta blew out a puff of air, anger turning her vision red. "Why did I talk to you about all this again?"

If Monica knew Loretta had insulted her, she chose to ignore it. "Because you needed to hear the truth, honey."

"Well, if I didn't mention it, thanks again."

Monica's hand patted the top of hers, not in an unkind way. "If I were you, I'd come down with my *own* sudden case of the flu, march over to his house, kick her skanky ass to the curb, and dump him proper."

The room started to spin, and Loretta put her other hand down on the desk to keep herself from falling. "Let's start with just finding out what's going on."

Monica shrugged. "Well, yeah, that's what I said. And tell him, from his co-workers, if *he* can't bother to call in, *we* can't bother to keep his job open."

The rush of dizziness passed, but Loretta felt worse than ever. She trudged toward the elevator.

By the time she dialed up the department supervisor, it took little acting on her part to feign sickness.

Chapter Seven

"Come on, Daryl. Stay with me, baby, what's wrong?" Maxine hovered over him, genuine concern reflected in her eyes.

Daryl sat, hunched over in the dining room chair, nibbling on a peanut butter sandwich she'd put together for him, telling himself he wasn't really dying, in spite of what his body told him. He had to focus and keep blinking to clear his vision of a watery scrim. He remembered catching a particularly nasty head cold one year where he spent a couple of days feeling disconnected with the world, like he viewed everything outside of himself. Seeing the world, dare he think it, ghostlike.

The same disconnection of not really being here overtook him now. *I just want to sleep.* But he'd already slept most of yesterday and a good part of the morning, and he felt worse than ever.

Maxine continued to encourage. "That's it; you need to eat, baby."

"I'm trying." As best he could tell, the goop in his mouth had no taste. He chewed mechanically, then stopped and closed his eyes as the room dipped and spun.

He hoped his strength would return just by forcing the food down. But as he ate, his stomach kept lurching. "Oh, God."

Somehow the fear of spewing on the carpet gave him the adrenaline burst to walk down the hall and into the bathroom, where he hurled the contents of his stomach into the toilet.

Stomach empty, he dry-heaved nasty bile that forced its way out his mouth until the tremors stopped. The smell of vomited nastiness spurred him to action so he wouldn't start hurling again.

He reached up, pulled the handle and closed his eyes, resting his head against the side of the bowl as he listened to the flushing cyclone rinse away the only nourishment he'd tried to keep down in the last several hours. *God, what am I going to do? What did I catch? I can't just...not eat!*

Somewhere above him, he heard water running from the sink tap, a soothing sound which settled his eyes shut. He almost drifted except for a coldness pressed against his face. He opened his eyes to see the pattern of the wadded damp washcloth brushing his face.

He closed his eyes again as Maxine crouched next to him, placing the cold cloth against the back of his neck. "Easy, Daryl. You're going to be just fine."

"I don't think so, Maxine." He reached up and dropped his arm across the back of her shoulders, gripping a handful of her shoulder strap with a clenched fist.

They rose together, and Maxine helped Daryl back to the dining room table. "Whatever I caught, I've never felt like this before. If this is a flu bug, it's a nasty one."

Maxine handed him the washcloth, and he dabbed at his face, trying to recover some sort of dignity after that messy display.

Daryl's spoke the next thought that entered his mind. "Maybe this is some sort of...ghost venereal disease."

"A what?"

"You know, like, a virus you get from having sex, but something from the ghost world." Blinking through a watery scrim, he couldn't quite read her blurry face.

But her tone communicated her dismissal just fine. "Don't be ridiculous, Daryl."

Daryl shook his head. "So says the ghost of Maxine Marie

standing in my dining room? We passed ridiculous in the rearview mirror some time ago, hon."

"You didn't catch a disease from me."

Daryl scoffed. "How do you *know* that? Ghosts don't come with free handbooks, you said. We don't know the rules. You said that yourself."

"Don't be cruel, Daryl."

Easy for her *to say. She's not the sick one.* Daryl pressed, "How do we know you're not emitting some sort of paranormal radiation that's making me sick?"

Maxine shot to her feet, sending her chair sprawling across the floor behind her. She swiped her hand at the table.

Shoved by the power of Maxine's mind, Daryl's plate flew across the room and bounced off the far wall.

She glared at him. "Oh, how typical. You don't want to understand me, so it's my fault! That's cruel, Daryl. All you need is some food and some fresh air and you'll be fine. You don't have to be cruel."

"I'm not being..." As he looked over, the waterworks had already started in the corners of her eyes. *She's trying to manipulate me again.* In his anger, he gave voice to his frustration. "Jesus, it's like talking to an eight-year-old!"

"*What* did you just say to me!"

Her hand clamped, vise-like, around his throat. At the same time, some sort of painful energy coursed through his body, causing his limbs to shake as spasms of pain seared over his skin.

She pulled him close, face-to-face, his vision dominated by her look of cruelty, her eyes flashing anger. "Don't you *ever* say *anything* like that to me again, mister!" Her hot breath spat in his face with each sneered syllable.

What the hell is she doing? His teeth rattled, and he forced words from his mouth as his body jerked and danced out of control. "Stop! Maxine, stop!"

"Apologize first!"

"You're hurting me." No sympathy in her eyes, no mercy in

her touch. The energy charge built up, grew more intense. And he knew she wouldn't stop. For the first time, he feared her.

"Apologize!"

"I'm sorry! Maxine, I'm sorry! Stop!"

The pain subsided, and Daryl dropped where she released him.

He found himself slumped over the table, the cold washcloth once again pressed against his neck. He realized he must have passed out, but her body pressed against his, fingers caressing, her voice whispering, trying to offer futile comfort. "I'm sorry, baby; I don't know what came over me. I'm so sorry. Please, get better, Daryl, please, I'm *so* sorry."

Words failed him. The shock of what just happened, the real danger she now posed if he spoke out against her, frightened him into silence. Instead, he reached out and patted her hand, the irony that he comforted her after what she had done was not lost on him. But what else could he do?

She continued in a chastising tone. "It's just...you sounded just like all the others before they'd leave me."

"Others?"

"When I was still alive. Before someone would leave, they'd belittle me, call me a child, and walk out the door. And I was helpless to stop them. And I'd be alone."

"Maxine..." He closed his eyes and counted slowly to five before he spoke. "What was that you just did to me?"

"I don't know, but isn't it *delicious*?" As he watched, her expression changed from sympathy to the look of someone very pleased with herself. "These things keep happening. I think I'm getting more powerful, Daryl. By the hour. By the minute!"

"Maxine, you need to control that...power, whatever it is."

"Oh, I'm okay now; I just sort of lost my head for a minute. But let's find you something to eat."

The doorbell rang.

Maxine glared at Daryl. "Who is it?"

Daryl shrugged. "I have no idea, Maxine." He rose from the

chair. His legs wobbled, but held him. He took a first step forward, and was relieved to find he could still walk.

"What are you doing?"

"I'm answering the door."

"But you can't! Then you'll want to leave me again!"

"I'm not going to—"

"Daryl Beasley, you open this door this minute or I'm coming in after you!" A wave of guilt and shock at hearing Loretta's angry bellow froze him mid-step. His mind went blank at the sound of her hurt and anger. "And I had *better* not find what I *think* I'm going to find!"

"Her!" Maxine hissed.

Shit! He found his voice and called out. "Wait, Loretta, I'm coming, don't..." And he heard the telltale metal rattling of the doorknob as a key inserted into it. *Oh, shit.*

The door flew open, and Loretta stood in the doorway, murder in her eyes.

Somehow, Daryl found the strength to step forward and lurch toward her. "Loretta, go now," he pleaded.

Loretta focused on Daryl, and her expression changed from anger to shock. "Oh, Daryl, my God, what happened to you?" She started toward him.

Then she saw the other figure in the room, and all sympathy vanished from her face.

Loretta's features reflected sadness personified. "Oh, I see. Oh, Daryl, you really *are* pathetic, aren't you?"

Daryl flailed his hands. "Loretta, it's not what you think—"

"Are you fucking her?"

The blunt question stopped him. "Loretta, that's kind of beside the point right now...."

"Because if you are, I'd say it's pretty much *exactly* what I think!"

"But, Loretta, this really *is* Maxine Marie."

Loretta shook her head. "Jesus, Daryl! When you asked me if I'd ever join you in a cosplay fantasy, I had no idea you'd take it this far just because I wasn't all for it. You should have just told me how important it was. You *should* have come to *me*."

"Loretta, it's not—"

"Where did you find her?"

Maxine cut in, the chill in her voice clear to Daryl. "Don't talk to him that way!"

Loretta scoffed. "Oh, that's great. She *sounds* like Maxine, too. Tell me, Daryl, does she stay in character when she's climaxing?"

"You don't want to mock me, little girl."

Words failed him. He could think of nothing he could do to diffuse this clusterfuck-in-the-making.

Loretta looked past Daryl now, addressing the "other woman" directly. "Oh, I'm sorry. I didn't realize Daryl splurged big money for a *professional*. Did you come with references, or did Daryl hold auditions?"

Daryl stepped toward her. "Loretta, please, don't."

He reached for her, but it was useless. With one hand, Loretta shoved him aside and stomped past him, hands balling into fists as she stomped across the floor toward Maxine.

As Loretta closed the distance, Maxine vanished, and Loretta passed through the space in the great room she'd occupied moments earlier.

As a mocking giggle hung in the air, Loretta turned, hands raised into fists.

Loretta's gaze met Daryl's, her puzzled concern apparent. "Daryl, what—"

Maxine phased in, her head bent back in a cackle before staring down Loretta with a challenge. "Daryl is mine, you stupid cow. Mine forever! You've lost him."

"What are you doing to him?" Loretta cried. She launched across the room, slamming into Maxine and dropping her to the ground. They fell in a heap in front of Daryl.

Shit! Go, Loretta! In their months of dating, Daryl had no idea Loretta was capable of such violence. *Maybe I've underestimated her.*

Loretta straddled Maxine, her hands entwined in Maxine's

hair. Maxine's teeth clenched in a growl, but she continued to giggle through it all.

Maxine gripped Loretta's forearms. Suddenly, Loretta's body shook and twitched, and Loretta's war cry turned to a scream of agony. Maxine's body vanished.

Loretta collapsed to the floor and dropped onto all flours. Beads of blood fell from her mouth and spotted the tile beneath her. "What, where..." She babbled and stared at the floor.

"No!" Daryl scrambled to his feet and grabbed Loretta by her shoulders, trying to pull her up. "Run, Loretta. Run now!"

Behind them, Maxine called out from the great room. "Daryl, darling, what are you doing?"

Daryl turned.

Maxine stood, essentially unhurt, arms raised. She looked upon them with venomous contempt. "Get away from her, Daryl. I have to do this. You know I have to. And you know you can't stop me, little man!"

"No!"

"Daryl?" Loretta whimpered. She still squatted on all fours, staring at the foyer tile where Daryl had shoved her forward.

Daryl crouched down next to her, talking into her ear. "Loretta. To your feet. Now. Run."

"But–"

"You can't stop her." He reached toward the door, turned the door handle and opened it. "Go, I'll keep her here, just go!"

Maxine screamed. "Out of my way, Daryl!"

Even as Loretta shuffled toward the opening, Maxine stepped toward them, a look of disgust on her face.

Daryl swallowed, steeled his courage, and pressed toward Maxine, raising his arms to block her.

Just as they would have collided, Maxine vanished.

"No!" Daryl spun on his heel.

An echo of an angry laugh floated toward the open door, closing in on Loretta.

Loretta had pressed forward on all fours. Now, halfway out the door, Maxine tackled her, her arms wrapped around Loretta's waist, her legs digging in, trying to pull her back. "Get back here, you stupid bitch!"

No, you don't Maxine! Daryl ran forward, wrapped his fingers into Maxine's hair, and shoved her face at the opening. As he hoped, the air sparked with static electricity, and Maxine was flung back into Daryl.

They both fell backward into the great room.

Daryl landed on the floor, head spinning. But he shook off his disorientation to sit up.

Loretta, now standing just outside the apartment, looked back at them through the frame of the open door.

Maxine appeared between them, waving her arms at Loretta. From the other side of the great room, the dining room chair flew over Daryl's head and into his line of sight, continuing toward the open door. *What?*

Maxine phased. The chair passed through her, still arcing in a deadly trajectory toward Loretta.

Daryl's heart caught in his throat.

Loretta stepped to the side. The chair flew past her and shattered on impact against the cement.

Thank God! "Run, Loretta! Now!"

Maxine sprinted to the apartment entrance. She thrust a hand, palm forward. The doorframe lit up in green static energy, forcing her back.

"Run, you stupid cow! Run! Don't ever come back! He's mine!"

With a final scream, Maxine pounded her fists against the energy barrier. She sank to her knees, watching from the entrance.

From where he lay, catching his breath, Daryl heard a familiar car engine turn over. In his mind's eye, he imagined Loretta in her car, pulling away, the car tires squealing across the parking lot as she peeled out.

She made it. Daryl let his head fall back on the carpet. The relief of knowing she'd gotten away had drained the last of his strength.

A moment later, she was there, crouching next to him, one

hand resting on his chest, and her eyes half-open in her most sexy stare. "It's not too late, Daryl," she spoke in her famous half-whisper.

"What?"

"It's not too late. Let me help you up. Just take the picture off the wall and take it outside. Then I can catch her." She raked her fingernails down the front of his T-shirt, trailing welts down the front of his T-shirt, painful enough to get his attention without causing agony.

Her point was clear: *I'm not hurting you. Yet.*

Daryl swallowed and braced himself. "No."

Her fingers froze mid-trail. Through his shirt, her nails pressed firm. Five pinpoints of lethal needles. "What?"

Daryl's body twitched under her touch, but he kept his voice firm. "You can't have her. Leave her out of this."

The moment hung between them for what seemed an eternity as both contemplated the consequences of what Daryl had said, of the choice he'd just made.

Maxine's face distorted into a grimace of fury. "You disappoint me, little man." Sparks of energy coursed through her hands and into his chest.

He closed his eyes. This was going to hurt.

Chapter Eight

LORETTA DROVE; her mind focused on one thought, to maneuver the car out of the parking lot, to get the hell away, and put as much distance between herself and that *creature* as fast as possible. Like a wild animal fleeing the lioness, her higher functions had disengaged; she operated at a level of reflex and response.

By the time she refocused on her surroundings, she was halfway home. She'd taken streets, maneuvered the route, all on automatic.

I got away. I'm safe. Somewhat safe. The creature can't get to me. Doesn't know where to find me. Daryl won't tell.

Blasts of instinctive imperatives smoothed out as her higher functions returned. *Okay, the creature is trapped within the apartment. It didn't chase me, though it clearly would have done so if it were capable. So it can't leave, and it has Daryl trapped in there with her.*

God, there's no way I can beat her without help, or at least without a plan. Without information. I was lucky just to get away.

Which is a good thing, because...

Then the shakes hit.

Loretta barely had time to ease the car into the shoulder and shift gears into park before the shakes overtook her. *That, that, whatever-she-is tried to kill me.* Would *have killed me, if Daryl hadn't stopped her.*

Loretta was not a violent person by nature. Sure, she'd been driven, *provoked,* to make a statement; to remove Maxine from Daryl by force. And if the little tramp refused to go quietly and took a black eye or a few bruises for her troubles, well, that was the cost of messin' with someone else's man. But for all her anger, as much as the betrayal hurt her, she would never have seriously hurt the woman. At least, not on purpose. She didn't think she had it in her. Maybe in a kill-or-be-killed situation, if she knew it going in.

But that isn't true of this creature. This, what is she? Ghost? Demon? Another creature altogether?

Maybe, just maybe, Daryl was forced, from the start. Maybe none of this is his fault.

But even as the thought entered her mind, she rejected it. No, that didn't fit the scenario. As much as she loved him, she also knew a real, living, in-the-flesh Maxine Marie would prove too tempting to him.

Tears poured down her face as she shook. The shakes intensified to tremors, getting worse instead of easing off. She tried to breathe it off, but the reality that she'd almost died made it impossible to function for now.

I just fought Maxine Marie. The real *Maxine Marie.* No question remained in Loretta's mind about that fact. Somehow, Maxine had returned to Earth in some spirit form, making her a...

Loretta had to steel herself before she could even *think* the word in any serious real-world context. *Making her a ghost.*

And yet, so much *more* than any sort of ghost of movies, legend, or TV show nonsense. She interacted in our world with neither restriction nor inhibition. Her ability to manipulate people and objects, to appear as flesh and blood. In the case of the kitchen chair, she had powers superior to a living person's. She was something more. Something more than Maxine Marie, something more than even the ghost of Maxine.

Loretta lifted her head from the driver's wheel as if she had just woken from a short nap. The irregular rhythm of the cars passing her by while they navigated rush hour traffic had lulled her, calmed her. Now she could think. Loretta needed help. She needed information, and she needed a plan. As she pondered the facts that frightened her into inaction, her mind boggled.

I can't go to the cops with this story!

I can't leave Daryl with her.

One other fact locked in her mind. Whatever happened, however it started, Daryl was in danger now. He needed her help desperately, and she needed to get him free from Maxine. Somehow, Daryl was still alive, but, given how he looked, she didn't think that would last long.

She had to think. She had to be smart about this. No, she couldn't go to the cops, but she *could* find the right people. She had a computer, and like any nerd girl with a social life, she had contacts with odd connections. It was time to use them.

With a next step in mind, she found the shakes had eased. With a little care, she thought she could drive home and start working those connections, to find out who knew who, until she found the person she needed to talk to.

Finally calm, she shifted the gear into drive and eased the car into the flow of traffic.

A GOOGLE SEARCH took her to a website called Ghost Woman Investigations.com, a local team of self-proclaimed ghost hunters. The team offered services for hire to clients to help screen locations and landmarks and confirm if any unexplained disturbances and episodes are indeed caused by a "paranormal presence" or to see if they can uncover a more mundane explanation.

It's a start. Loretta hit the chat button and left a message for someone to contact her as soon as possible.

She left the chat window open and sat back in her chair. Who else could she call? What else could she do? She opened a new tab in her browser and started surfing the web for other ghost encounters and hauntings throughout the world, and she found herself dissatisfied with the results. "Hauntings" by typical description culminated into a cluster of anecdotal eyewitness reports detailing uncertain visions, noises, sightings of lights, cold spots; ambiguous encounters at best.

And no reports online amounted to someone directly conversing in a dialog exchange with a ghost, and certainly nothing about coming to physical blows with creatures that demonstrated both the power and the inclination to fling large objects at the living when provoked.

Just for good measure, she typed in "Maxine Marie Ghost." Google returned sets of quotes, short vignettes about grieving friends and relatives of the movie star, most of them lamenting about whether the ghost of Maxine might be smiling down in approval of some tribute, or how some current generation actress seemed to be channeling the ghost of Maxine in their latest role.

But nothing equating to anyone who encountered an actual presence that claimed to be the famous icon, back from the dead with her sights set on stealing someone's boyfriend.

No, my *boyfriend had to be the first to crack* that *nut. Lucky me.*

It was her worst fear personified. She was well aware that Daryl's infatuation for Maxine stemmed from the fact the Maxine fit the gold standard of what he considered the physical ideal, the "perfect ten," every detail checked, every proportion made to order. Stacked against that, Loretta's physical reality fell short of the ideal.

Her dark red hair would not dye blonde easily, even if she felt inclined to cave to such shallow criteria, which she did not. Loretta's fairly straight strands lacked the oceanic wave of Daryl's idol. Maxine's figure flared out into large full breasts, nipped in to a flat waistline before curving back out into the world's most famous figure eight, a figure against which all other bodies were since compared and found lacking. Loretta could never firm up her tummy to that extent. Though, according to most biographies,

Maxine herself struggled to maintain her own standard throughout her short, famous life.

But it shouldn't have mattered. After all, in all things that *did* matter: the ability to offer warm, sexual affection, to interact, to respond and return attention, and bond in a *real* way, certainly trumped any fantasy. This reality helped Loretta bear with the "competition" for all these months. But now...

She'd been competing against the real thing, and she didn't even know it.

Overnight, Daryl had become so smitten, so overwhelmed, so *satisfied* by what must have been a brief interlude, that he couldn't bring himself to tell Loretta the truth. Instead, he chose to just end their relationship and then risk his job and very livelihood so he could stay home with her and engage in God-knows-what.

And yet, something wasn't right. Daryl didn't look just tired in a "shagged out from too much sex" kind of way, he looked unhealthy. Starved.

Daryl was in trouble. Serious trouble. Every instinct told her so.

Her computer beeped an alert, and her chat window flashed a new message,

Renee: Hello, Loretta. Sorry to keep you waiting. My name is Renee.

Loretta started typing, her fingers flying over the keyboard, typing as fast as she could think the thoughts.

Visitor: I have a sort of paranormal emergency, and need expert help as fast as possible.

Renee: Interesting, Loretta. By emergency, do you mean persistent visitations, knockings, flashes of light, other disturbances that need investigating?

Loretta paused, considering. "Disturbances" didn't even begin to cover it.

Visitor: No, this has gone far beyond that. These are positive visitations and an ongoing incident involving two-way interaction and...

She considered.

...contact from a paranormal source with intent to cause physical injury.

Renee: That hardly seems likely, Loretta. Can you describe the phenomenon?

Loretta hesitated.

Visitor: I'm afraid it's going to sound a bit outlandish. It's why I don't want to go to the police, but coming to you instead.

Renee: That's okay, Loretta. Just tell me what evidence you've uncovered while encountering the phenomenon.

As she typed, Loretta rolled her eyes. *This might prove a huge mistake, but I've gone too far. I have to trust someone.*

Visitor: I was physically assaulted and forcibly ejected from a residence by a supernatural presence that clearly demonstrated powers beyond human ability.

Loretta tapped her fingers against the wooden desktop for almost three minutes before a response appeared on her screen.

Renee: If I understand you correctly, your needs are less about investigation and confirmation of a phenomenon, but more about seeking knowledge on how to remove or contain an openly aggressive paranormal presence?

Loretta considered.

Visitor: Is such a thing possible?

Again, she waited through a long pause.

Renee: Yes, but not by us.

A sick deflating sensation in her gut caused the words to blur on her screen. *God, now what?* She typed,

Visitor: Do you know anyone who can help me?

Renee: Hold on just a moment.

Loretta waited much longer than a moment. Her stomach churned and the backs of her eyes burned from a stress headache. *I'm stressed. Go figure. I may have just wasted precious time I don't have.*

Finally, the screen beeped, and a new message appeared.

Renee: Can I assume you need extraction as soon as possible?

Loretta swallowed.

Visitor: Yes.

Renee: Very well. Please fill out the contact form on this page and include your cell phone number. Stay by your phone. Someone will contact you shortly.

LORETTA DIDN'T DRINK OFTEN, but she kept at least one bottle of dessert wine on hand so she'd be prepared for any upcoming special occasions. Valentine's Day, Christmas, whatever. She'd mentally tagged the current bottle of chocolate raspberry merlot chilling in the back of the fridge for her birthday, with plans to take it to Daryl's apartment next week and share it while she opened her presents, and then, being in an exceptionally good mood, thank him *very much*. Halfway through the bottle, it didn't exactly drown her sorrows, but she no longer wanted to cry. That was something.

In spite of the buzz, her head cleared the moment her cell phone erupted into the chorus of "E.T." by Katy Perry. Loretta took in the words "Blocked Number" and stabbed the talk button before Katy could finish begging the alien to "t-t-take" her.

"Loretta Stevens?" A woman's voice.

Loretta's throat turned bone-dry, and her mind blanked. She tilted the receiver away from her mouth, sipped at the wine, and tried again. "Y-yes."

"My name is Rebecca Burton. Renee Johnson contacted me. I'm a freelance agent for the Indiana Special Investigations Unit. I understand you have a need for a consultation with an expedient turnaround?"

An occasional science fiction convention-goer, (Daryl and Loretta had attended the last local Gen Con and Starbase Indy together) Loretta considered her "weird-ar" fairly attuned. The voice on the other end sounded professional, grounded, and held none of the shaky, erratic tones that signaled a quack-pot.

Still, the information didn't click. "What sort of investigations did you say you do again?"

"I investigate paranormal and other phenomenon throughout Indiana, Ms. Stevens."

"But that's not what you said."

"I said I was a state employee in the Special Investigations department, Ms. Stevens. You might be interested to know there are over forty such units throughout the United States."

"There are?"

The voice on the other end laughed. "We're sort of an open secret. If you take a step back from your current dilemma, what would be your response to knowing your government supported a paranormal and unexplained phenomenon division?"

"I suppose..." Loretta considered. "I'd think it an irresponsible waste of time and taxpayers' money."

"Exactly, Ms. Stevens. So our biggest challenge is to make the department services available to those who need us, while hiding in plain sight from those who don't understand, or refuse to acknowledge, the need for us. If you're interested, I'll guide you to our department webpage on Indiana.gov. It's rather bare-bones, but most clients feel much better seeing proof that we're the result of your tax dollars at work."

Loretta clicked the address bar of her web browser. "Please."

Burton rattled off the address. And there it was, on the Indiana.gov site, a simple listing of the Special Investigations Unit personnel directory (three names, including Agent Rebecca Burton) and their extensions from the main city office number.

Loretta released a deep sigh. *I'm not losing my mind, and I haven't contacted a crackpot.*

Still all business, Burton droned on. "Now, if I understand your situation correctly, your need is rather immediate. Tell me, are you close to the Café Expresso in Broad Ripple?"

"That's about fifteen minutes from my apartment."

"Perfect, Ms. Stevens. I'll meet you there in one hour. Please be prepared to be one-hundred percent forthcoming about your situation. Rest assured, I'll do all I can to help you."

<h1 style="text-align:center">Chapter Nine</h1>

LORETTA ENTERED the coffee shop and stood in the foyer while her eyes adjusted to the darkness. She'd driven past the shop many times since moving to Indy, but, with her college years long behind her, had no reason to stop and visit, especially with a branch of her favorite coffee place across the street from InfoTech.

The sprawling seating room, adorned with light-colored wood panels and dark oak trim, created an atmosphere more akin to a pub or winery than a coffee shop. Still, the aroma of fresh coffee permeated the room to a stifling extent. Loretta imagined her brain perking up with each inhale.

Directly in front of her, a long bar extended across the room. Beneath the wood counter were partitioned bins of clear plastic filled with coffee beans lined up, side by side, like various treats in a candy store. Labels identified a plethora of choices: The Expresso Special; The Inspiration; The Poet Primer; Morning Glory, and so on.

A woman behind the counter withdrew a scoop of fine beans from the Morning Glory bin and poured the contents into one of the espresso machines.

Three college-aged customers sat on stools at the bar, their laptops open on the counter. Round tables and booths circled the bar. In observance of the "Please Seat Yourself" sign in the foyer, Loretta worked her way to a booth in the corner where she could see the entrance.

A waitress approached.

Loretta decided caffeine would be a good counter to the alcohol she'd consumed. She also needed more chocolate. So she ordered café mocha and waited for her contact.

A tall woman with striking, long red hair entered. Her calf-length black leather trench coat and black brimmed hat reminded Loretta of a character from a 1940s *film noir*. The woman's serious, dignified demeanor made the style work for her.

Loretta knew, without question, the woman was Rebecca Burton. If Burton's intention was to blend in, she'd failed. Everything about her screamed, "G-man" or, actually, "G-woman."

Even shadowed by the hat, the agent's eyes scanned the room with a piercing gaze. She locked on Loretta, nodded at her, and approached the booth.

Burton extended a hand. "Ms. Stevens?"

Loretta took it. As Burton pumped her hand once and released, Loretta noted her palm felt soft, but firm.

Burton took a seat across from her, and, in a fluid motion, raised her hand, lifted the hat off her head, and placed it down on the empty space in the booth.

Burton shook her head. The motion allowed her red hair (much brighter than Loretta's auburn strands) to billow out around her head. The display came off both practiced and natural.

The brim of the hat had hidden sharp green eyes, but, in Loretta's opinion, Burton was much younger than her impression of the agent over the phone. Loretta sensed Burton was willing, almost *eager*, to help. She judged the woman to be in her early to mid-twenties. In either case, Loretta turned thirty-three next week, and Burton looked like a kid in comparison.

Burton flicked a business card at the table.

Out of reflex, Loretta picked it up and read it, "Rebecca Burton, Independent Agent, Special Investigations Unit." The website address followed, along with an Indiana.gov email address. The left half of the card displayed the generic state logo popping out in embossed black. Loretta rubbed her thumb over the impression.

"So you really are a government agent."

Rebecca offered a quick nod. "Yes, though technically, I'm a contractor for the state. This allows me certain...flexibility to pursue all areas of the paranormal, including many that fall outside the interest to the state."

Loretta grinned. "So you're a ghostbuster for hire."

Rebecca considered. "Something like that. The goals of the state align with many of my goals. But I have access to additional resources, which I freely share when the need arises."

Unsure where to begin, Loretta asked, "So, as an agent for Indiana Special Investigations, how can you help me today?"

"Our department investigates paranormal and supernatural activity of a potentially alarming nature with the objective of containing or eradicating the situation. We also spin the media about the supernatural episode. Should I find your case qualifies, I'll ask you to sign a statement to the effect that you waive your right to blog, mention through social media, or contact anyone connected with a media outlet to discuss your encounter, including television, radio, and print. Nor can you write a book about it, or speak about it to anyone." Agent Burton's smile broke her stoic demeanor, warming her face. "In most cases, this isn't a problem. Not many people want to go on record about their encounters with the supernatural."

Loretta nodded. "The last thing I need is for people to find out I'm losing my boyfriend to the ghost of a '60s bombshell. Still, isn't this secrecy questionable?"

Agent Burton shook her head. "The government has many reasons to minimize incidences of this nature. Beyond the waste of time from skeptics who insist on reopening each case for further validation, the current national policy is that it's not in the best interest of the public to know the magnitude of supernatural episodes throughout the country, or the world, for that matter. Can you imagine the alarm that knowledge would cause?"

Though stated in a matter-of-fact manner, the implications left her chilled. "Aren't you taking a terrible risk telling me that?"

Burton smiled, fixing her with a coy expression. "The paperwork is a formality, Ms. Stevens. You won't tell anyone."

Befuddled, Loretta stewed on this simple statement. *She's right, but how can she be so confident? Does she have some way to wipe my mind, like the memory eraser device in* Men in Black?

Something else clicked with Loretta. "Wait, you told me you have agents in...did you say forty states?"

The waitress deposited an insulated cup on the table. "What can I get you, Rebecca?" she said in a husky voice. She waited with a pen and order pad in hand.

Burton flashed a smile. "Espresso, double."

"The usual? You got it." The waitress walked off.

Agent Burton reached into the folds of her jacket, produced a clam-shaped mini-laptop, and pried it open on the table between them. "I think it's time we discussed your case in detail, Ms. Stevens."

Loretta lifted the cup to her lips. The strong cocoa-java aroma broke through some of her confusion and left her head buzzing. "Wait a second. Don't dodge my question. Does this sort of shit happen all over the place?" As her tongue touched the blazing-hot liquid, she pulled the cup back. *Ouch!*

"I'm not free to discuss the full parameters of such episodes, Ms. Stevens." Burton leaned over the tiny screen of her laptop. "What I am *also* saying is that I have resources and information that can be invaluable in helping you. But, in exchange for that help, you need to be less curious about matters that don't concern to you."

Loretta resigned herself to holding the cup under her nose and enjoying the aroma of the fumes until her coffee cooled enough to drink. "You're practically telling me that this sort of thing is going on all the time?"

Burton looked down at her laptop. "These incidents are not as widespread as you make it sound, Ms. Stevens." The glow from her screen lit up her face in an odd blue tint. Her striking red hair dulled to copper color. "Odds are, once we've wrapped up this particular misadventure, you won't experience a situation like it for the rest of your life."

Loretta raised her hand in a stopping motion. "The Ms. Stevens address sounds condescending."

Burton dipped her chin in another brief nod. "Fair enough, Loretta. And you may call me Rebecca. The title Agent Burton draws a lot of attention."

The waitress returned with a second coffee cup and the receipt, depositing both at Rebecca's elbow. She gave Rebecca a wink before turning away. Loretta wondered what that was about, but decided it wasn't her business. *I need help. And she's offering to help me.*

Rebecca glanced down at the computer screen and began typing.

As the silence extended, Loretta waited, repressing the urge to fidget.

Rebecca met Loretta's gaze. "Now, why don't you start at the beginning and tell me the whole story?"

Loretta thought back. *Where to begin?* "Well, it started three days ago. I was supposed to meet Daryl at his apartment, so we could go shopping for my birthday present."

"Oh, yes, your birthday is next week."

Loretta couldn't hide her surprise. "That's correct, but how did you know that?"

"I'm a government agent, Loretta. Happy early birthday."

"Oh...of course. Well, thank you." *This is going to take some getting used to.*

"Don't mention it. Go on."

Loretta told her story, going through the incident at the souvenir store in detail.

Rebecca asked several follow up questions, fixating on the odd way Daryl's card slipped from his hand.

Finally, Loretta reached the part where she'd stormed off and boarded the bus.

Rebecca asked, "You took a public IndyGo bus?"

"Yes. And I rode it to Daryl's apartment and drove home. Except..."

Rebecca looked up from the screen, and one eyebrow rose. "Yes?"

Loretta smiled, amused. Burton's expression reminded her of Spock from *Star Trek*. Out loud, she said, "Something strange happened on the bus."

Rebecca nodded. "I was about to ask."

"The man I sat next to, an old, short man with an accent, said something."

"Scottish accent?" Loretta noticed Rebecca's inflection of interest.

"I think so. He called himself the travel king or something like—"

"The Transit King?"

"Yes. That was it. How did you know?"

"Interesting." Rebecca typed for several seconds. "Very interesting. How did he address you?"

"Well," Loretta rubbed her head. The headache threatened to return, and her coffee was still too hot. "He said he knew I was in trouble and that I should wait for Daryl in the apartment rather than go home."

"And did you?"

"No, but what do you know about this Transit King guy?"

"Well..." Burton looked off to the side. "Not much. He knows a lot about paranormal events throughout the city. He seems well attuned to them." Rebecca took a gulp of her beverage. "In the past, he's approached our department to offer information, and, in my experience, his leads always pan out."

"So, do you think if I'd listened to this Transit King and stayed with Daryl, things might have gone differently?"

Rebecca frowned. "It's hard to say. My guess is you might have delayed what happened, rather than prevented it. Or, upon seeing you and Daryl together, the ghost might have moved on, and I'd be having this discussion with someone else, *if* that someone was able to get in touch with me."

Loretta took another experimental sip from her mocha. Very tasty, and no longer scalding hot. "So, note to self, if I ever meet this Transit King guy again, I should do what he says."

"Maybe."

Loretta gave a mental shrug at the cryptic comment. She told the rest of what happened as best as she understood it.

Rebecca listened without further interruption or insight.

When Loretta finished, Rebecca said, "Daryl is Maxine's most immediate source of power. She has access to his thoughts and desires."

"You mean she feeds off him?"

"It may not be as purposeful as that, but it fits the events. And another thing is certain; the rent check is the anchor."

That makes sense. Loretta closed her eyes against the pain building up behind her eyeballs. The coffee, though delicious, didn't help in the least. "So what do we do?"

"We have to destroy the check. Completely."

"So we have to break in and somehow get hold of the check?" Loretta didn't like that news at all. "Can't we just, I don't know, get a Catholic priest to say a prayer outside the apartment door? Wave around some incense, sprinkle holy water, and do the sign of the cross?"

Rebecca smiled. "Perhaps as an optional secondary strategy."

"Would it help?"

"No. Destroying the check is the answer." Rebecca leaned away from the laptop. "The good news is that, typically, a spirit can't manipulate the anchor object through its own power. Only living people can move or manipulate the object the spirit is bound to. Spirits are also contained within the property grounds of the possessor of those objects."

"But this is an apartment."

Burton shrugged. "Apparently, that distinction doesn't matter. Which means, as long as Daryl keeps the check in the apartment, Maxine can't leave. That's why she didn't chase you outside. She couldn't."

"But if someone took the check outside the property?"

Rebecca nodded. "Then the spirit can roam freely."

"Well, thank goodness that Daryl..."

The truth of what happened hit Loretta like a physical blow. A sickening queasiness cramped her stomach. "Daryl...shoved me outside, to get me out of her reach. He saved me. Sacrificed himself and stayed behind. That means he's Maxine's only way to move the check."

"That could be good for him. She still has to keep him alive."

The danger Daryl was in made Loretta's heart ache.

Rebecca reached over and touched Loretta's arm. "Are you okay?"

"God, he looked so horrible. You should have seen him." She thought of Daryl's sunken face, the look of despair in his dark eyes, and she felt dizzy. The room dimmed to near black.

Rebecca slid the palm of her hand in a comforting motion down Loretta's arm to grasp her hand. A warm, tingling sensation traveled into Loretta's palm and up her arm, soothing her fear. Her mind felt somewhat clearer. *I need to stay focused. Daryl needs me.*

Rebecca's hand tightened on Loretta's.

Something happened. Something deep inside "flushed" though Loretta and settled her thoughts. The churning in her stomach eased; the panicked thoughts stopped colliding in her head.

"Be still," Rebecca whispered. Her voice seemed to reach Loretta from a great distance. Rebecca closed her eyes. "I can see you love him very much."

The agent's touch burned and soothed and comforted all at once.

With the release of her pain came a welling of pent-up emotion. *No, I don't want to....*

A voice spoke in her mind. *Peace.*

We don't have time to....

Peace!

Tears poured down Loretta's face, twin streams of emotion that trickled out of her. "Please save him. Please. I know he and I will need to face what he did, but I just want him safe."

"Shhhh." Rebecca opened her eyes, and their gazes met. "He's very lucky to have you. We're going to do all we can. You have to believe that."

"I do."

Rebecca released her, and, like a faucet turned off, the coursing energy stopped.

Loretta dabbed at her cheeks with her napkin and then blew her nose. She settled back in her chair and took a deep breath. The coffee shop snapped into sharp focus. Her thoughts came to her clearly, organized and calm. For the first time since this nightmare began, Loretta felt like herself.

"That's better." Rebecca smiled at her. "Let me continue. Most paranormal creatures struggle to manipulate even small objects. Most can't keep a material form for more than a few seconds. To render herself solid enough to...interact as you described, indicates extraordinary control and a siphoning of enormous ecto-energies."

Loretta stared at her, slack-jawed. "Ecto-what?"

"Consider." Rebecca indicated her coffee cup. "Let's say this is Maxine Marie. Once she died, she left the physical realm and entered another realm that exists congruent to ours on a plane our senses can't normally detect."

Rebecca held out her hand, palm flat, turned sideways against the cup. "She's there, but people can't see her. Maxine Marie must gather enough ecto-energy to punch though back into our realm." She lifted her hand and then dropped it again. "It takes energy to break through, and even more energy to *stay*. That's why so many spirits can only make themselves known for a moment at a time."

"What form does this ecto-energy take?"

Rebecca considered. "One popular theory says ghosts convert mental and psychic energy from humans into ecto-energy. For example, when a psychic medium gathers a group of mourners, they direct everyone to focus on memories of the dearly departed. The communal thoughts create a concentration of energy, so the spirit can sometimes break through and make contact."

Loretta rubbed her hands together, hopeful to trigger a

residual afterglow from their encounter. "You mean, like, moving an Ouija board, or cold spots, or levitating small objects? All the typical ghost activity?" She considered the enduring worldwide popularity of Maxine Marie. "Do we know if ecto-energy needs to be localized?"

Rebecca grabbed for her coffee and took a drink, a thoughtful look on her face. "I don't think there's any proof one way or the other." She shrugged. "Ecto-energy itself is just a working theory."

"Well, there you have it." Loretta spread her hands out. "If memories, thoughts, ideas, celebrations of, compassion for...if any time a person thinks about a spirit, if that's potential energy, and that energy remains untapped over a period of time...Rebecca, Maxine died almost fifty years ago."

Rebecca's finger's drummed against the tabletop, the closest reaction akin to excitement Loretta had witnessed during their time together. "And her fame has multiplied during that time. She's now an icon of '50s and '60s Americana. Add to that, decades of movie exhibitions, who knows how many published biographies, a thriving fan base scrambling to find memorabilia, and a profitable estate feeding that frenzy with posters, pictures, pinups, special magazine issues, YouTube videos; thousands and thousands of fans and admirers thinking about her at any point of any day—"

"Rebecca, younger fans still think of her in her prime, her sexual prime." Loretta's voice cracked. "And by younger fans, that could mean anyone under age sixty. Men fantasize about her like they would any other *living* person, or movie star. Very few of those fans let the fact of her death distract them. Not the way you mourn a loved one. Normal people just don't fantasize about the dead."

Rebecca made a face. "One would hope very few."

"Yes, but that's not true in Maxine's case." Loretta grabbed Rebecca's arm. "She's fair game. She devoted her life to being a sex fantasy to the men of the world, women too. And I don't just mean lesbians. I mean, she's still a template for women who want to be sexually adventurous, who want a role model on how to keep things exciting in the bedroom."

Loretta finished, "And sexual fantasies are the basic, most primal, thoughts. How much ecto-power would fifty years of that sort of intensity give her?"

Rebecca withdrew a sheet of paper from her jacket. "We need to hurry." She extended the folded sheet of paper along with an ink pen. "Sign it."

"What's this?"

"The contract I mentioned earlier. In essence, it says this case is officially top secret, and any breach of this confidentiality will result in prosecution, up to and including throwing you into the deepest hole in Saudi Arabia."

Loretta stared at her. "Saudi Arabia?"

Rebecca grinned. "I'm kidding, of course. We have plenty of deep holes here in the States. Sign here."

Loretta looked at the contract, barely registering the tiny legalese.

Without another thought, she scribbled her name on the contract and picked up the credit card receipt.

Chapter Ten

As if from a great distance, Maxine's voice reached him. "Daryl, wake up, *please* wake up!"

He opened his eyes to look into her pale face.

She'd pulled him into a sitting position, leaning him against the couch. Now, she kneeled in front of him, examining his face, her half-opened eyes reflecting worry.

He waited in the tense silence for her to say something, to offer to get help, to try to cook something. Anything.

Instead, she moved toward his side and curled up against him.

Her touch revolted him. He tried to push away, but he was too weak to move. "I'm here, Maxine, but I don't know how much longer."

Through the window, he could see the porch and the lake beyond it in the bright sunlight. The view did nothing to warm him, or make him feel better. Given the lack of strength in his limbs, he figured this would be the last thing he'd see. He looked over at the creature responsible for his fate. He couldn't even summon up the energy to properly hate her for what she had done to him. He no longer thought of her as Maxine Marie, the sexy starlet back from the dead, the childlike woman who just wanted to love and be loved. As she'd fed off his adoration of her, she'd somehow turned into a creature drunk on power, with no one to answer to.

But now, she gazed upon him with a look of compassion. "Daryl, you look terrible, honey. Here, drink this." When she spoke to him with such tenderness, he had hope. Now, in this moment of lucidity, perhaps he could reach her.

She brought a glass to his lips.

He tried to swallow, but the water poured down his throat and forced a coughing spasm.

She looked upon him with what appeared to be genuine concern. "We need to get you help. You won't last much longer if you keep up like this."

No shit. Even on the verge of death, he had little patience for statements of the obvious. Out loud, he said, "You should have...thought of that...before you attacked me, Maxine."

"Don't say that, Daryl. You won't die if you let me help you. Just grab the picture and take it outside. I'll get you help."

In spite of his dire circumstance, Daryl laughed. "I couldn't...walk now...even if I wanted to, Maxine. I can't even move. But more to the point, I wouldn't take the picture outside...even if I could!"

"But, Daryl, I could get help."

"Or you'd go after Loretta."

"No, no I wouldn't Daryl, I swear! I'd go straight to a hospital and get help."

A laugh escaped from him, causing fresh pain in his abdomen. Unimportant, under the circumstances. "Fair...enough, Maxine. You don't need to...get help. My cell phone...is on the desk over there. You can dial 9-1-1 and send for help."

Maxine's lower lip protruded.

Daryl knew what she'd say before he heard the words.

"Of course, my darling Daryl...*after* you move the picture outside."

"I *can't.*"

"You mean you won't! All because of that...that *person* you think you still love."

"Maxine, I can barely move right now, let alone get my legs under me."

"I don't believe you!" She sneered. "But if that's true, then at least it will be easier for you to die than it was for me. I was alone."

The sneer vanished from her face, and she pulled him to her in a hug. "Whatever happens, you won't die alone. I'll be right here. I promise." Warm, tender lips brushed against his cheek, but did little to distract him from the bitter feelings about his own impending death. He shuddered, revolted by her kiss.

"Maxine, it doesn't have to come to that. Just bring me—"

The doorbell rang.

MAXINE GLARED AT DARYL. A part of her was sick with worry over him. She really didn't want him to die. But another part didn't trust Daryl any more than she trusted any man once she'd been betrayed. *What are you up to now? Oh, how I wish I could read your mind, you crafty bastard.* "Who is that?"

"How should I know? It could be a Jehovah's Witness?"

"What the hell is a—"

This time whoever-it-was knocked hard, insistent. "Open up, please! I need to speak with Daryl Beasley on urgent corporate business!"

Maxine's mind spun. *What to do?* "Okay, Daryl. Looks like help has maybe arrived. You go along with me, and maybe I'll get you the help you need. Okay?"

Daryl nodded.

Maxine didn't think he had the strength to cry out, not after what had happened. Not that she meant to be so rough, but Daryl had been so naughty!

Maxine rose, checked herself. She still wore the same yellow sundress, fairly rumpled, hardly professional, but hardly scandalous, either. As she approached the door, she ran her hands through her hair.

She cleared her throat. "Sorry, who did you say this was?"

"Rebecca Burton from InfoTech, ma'am. I'm from Health and Human Resources. We haven't heard from Mister Beasley in three days, and they asked that we check up on him. Standard procedure."

Maxine's head spun. *Standard procedure? Do they do that in corporate offices?* She answered herself. *How would I know? I haven't had a desk job in sixty years! It sounds logical. I told Daryl to call in.*

She reached out. To her relief, her hand wasn't shocked when she turned the doorknob, and the door swung inward. A tall professional woman in a most *elegant* leather jacket stood on the other side. A pair of reflective sunglasses covered her eyes.

As Maxine adjusted to the bright sunlight, the woman flashed a pocketbook wallet with a card she didn't have time to read before folding it shut. "Health and Human Resources, miss. And you are?"

"Uh...Smith. Nurse Maxine Smith." Maxine dropped into improvisational acting mode, drawing upon techniques she learned in classes she'd attended a couple years before she'd died. *Observe, listen to the other actor, and deliver your lines with confidence.* "Mister Beasley's doctor assigned me to stay with him. The doctor called me after examining Daryl, Mister Beasley that is, here in the apartment. Didn't he call you?"

The human resources woman lowered her glasses to look directly upon Maxine with her sharp green-eyed stare. Her light red eyebrows rose. "Good to meet you, Nurse Smith. Did I under-stand you correctly? You say Mister Beasley's doctor made a *house call?*"

What did I say wrong? "Beasley is a special case. His doctor is his...brother-in-law."

Burton smiled. "And are you also a relative? You look like you've been here quite some time."

Maxine released a held breath. *She bought it!* "No, I—"

"Look, nurse, what I really need is his signature and his

doctor's signature on this release form by tomorrow, or things could go badly for him at work." Rebecca held a set of folded papers out at her side. "Can you fax these to us in that amount of time?"

"Can I what?" Maxine blinked, pretending to consider. *What's a facts?*

"Can you fax them, Nurse Smith?"

"Uh...certainly. I mean, I think so."

She waited, but the woman never extended the papers, just held them near her side as if expecting Maxine to step out onto the porch.

But I can't. Maxine considered, and knew the answer. She really needed to get Daryl medical attention, even if she couldn't go with them. "On second thought, Ms. Burton, I was getting ready to call the doctor myself. Maybe you'd like to come in and see what you think. We may need to get him some help."

"I'd be happy to, Nurse Smith."

As the woman stepped into the foyer, Maxine heard a noise behind her.

Maxine spun in time to see *her*, the stupid cow, standing across the room, raising the picture frame with the canceled check up over her head.

PROPPED AGAINST THE COUCH, Daryl listened to the exchange, trying to figure out what was going on. He didn't recognize the woman by her voice. And why would InfoTech send someone from HR to his house? It didn't make sense.

The room spun, and his head fell back onto the couch cushion.

A movement on the patio caught his attention. His eyes focused on a figure peering into the glass door, hands on either side to cut back the glare.

Loretta!

Her eyes widened in recognition, and her face showed her concern. She raised a finger to her lips.

No, Loretta! But he could barely make a sound, let alone shout a warning.

Loretta reached toward the handle, slid the patio door halfway open, and stepped in. Her gaze darted to the wall over the television, specifically, his shrine to all things Maxine Marie. With one quiet step across the carpet, she closed the distance, reached out, and placed her hands on the picture frame containing the check. She lifted it up, trying to clear the nail it hung upon.

The picture slid along the rough-white wall, making a loud scraping noise.

Loretta pulled the picture from the wall and started to lift it high, her look of fury telegraphing her desire to smash it to bits.

"Bitch!" Maxine Marie closed the distance, propelling across the room at supernatural speed, hitting Loretta in a running tackle.

Loretta and Maxine slammed against the sliding door, and the glass exploded. Shards flew everywhere.

They landed in a tangled heap. A shower of deadly sharp crystals rained down over them, slicing through cloth and flesh.

Daryl struggled to move, to go to Loretta. But, no matter how much he strained his muscles, they wouldn't cooperate. He could only stare, helpless.

Chapter Eleven

Maxine recovered quickly and raised herself to her hands and knees. Glass like deadly diamonds poured over her, slicing her arms and legs. She stared down at the porch, watching the shards sprinkle over the wood surface along with dotted drops of her blood.

Rather than anger, she enjoyed the pain. *I'm bleeding. I can bleed! I'm flesh and blood. And so much more.*

She grinned, giving herself over to the *delicious* ecstasy of pain.

Something bit her cheek, her arms; shards of glass dug into her knees. The stinging fresh pain sharpened her senses, rejuvenated her, aroused her. *I'm through the glass! I'm outside!*

As the spray of deadly daggers settled, her vision centered on her adversary. A growl vibrated the back of her throat. Maxine watched her enemy crawling, struggling to pull herself across the porch, leaving her own fresh trails of blood. Loretta's fear wafted over to her.

Maxine absorbed it, and her body responded with a rush of pleasure.

The overpowering instinct took over. *Taunt Loretta; prolong her suffering! Taste her fear; it's so* delicious, *isn't it? The best is yet to come!*

The more Loretta struggled, the more Maxine could *smell* her fear, feed upon her desperation, absorb it through her skin, like an aphrodisiac. Maxine's body quivered in response, building to something familiar, yet alien, driven by a compulsion beyond human needs.

I...like it!

Loretta reached out a hand toward the picture.

Maxine's fingers scraped against the wood of the deck, waiting. *Now! Now! No, wait! Her pain will taste so much more* delicious *if I wait just a moment more! Play possum until the perfect moment. Let her think she might succeed. Then, pounce.*

Loretta's fingers touched the edge of the frame.

Now!

Maxine leapt, slamming into Loretta, knocking her victim off the porch and sending her sprawling in the grass.

Maxine moans of pleasure mingled with Loretta's cries of pain. "Oh, you stupid cow, I underestimated you...you're *fantastic*!"

How long can I do this? Minutes? Hours?

Loretta rolled to find her footing, the picture frame just out of reach. She pulled her knees under her. As a shard of glass tore her upper thigh, she cried out.

Oh, God, she's bleeding! Yes! A flushing response coursed through Maxine's body. *I'm so...close! More, baby!*

Loretta growled, stood on wobbly legs, and drew her fist back.

Maxine waited, smiling, unmoving.

"Sick bitch!" Loretta smashed Maxine in the mouth.

Maxine's head rocked back from the impact. She dropped to her knees, blinking through the pain coursing through her head. She tasted her blood and spat at the ground, and then squatted at the spot where she'd fallen, watching through half-closed eyes, unable to keep a smile from forming.

Loretta shuffled toward the picture, her efforts forcing a moan from her. She scooped up the frame once again, clutching it between her hands.

Maxine raised a hand, commanding the winds to stir. A hard

blast of air gusted from her, slamming into Loretta, like a punch to the gut.

The wind pitched Loretta into the air and sent her flying toward the pond. Her scream of outrage and surprise were mostly lost to the wind.

The frame flipped from her fingers and fell on the ground.

Loretta slammed into the water, her scream cut off mid-cry.

Satisfaction coursed through Maxine.

The frame bounced off the ground, landing face-up near Maxine's feet. The spider web of a fresh break marred the face of the picture. *Stupid cow; she did that!*

Loretta's head broke the surface of the water, a growl of animal fury issued from her throat. Her hands curled into fists.

Maxine waved a hand.

A burst of water exploded in Loretta's face. She stumbled, blinded and blinking.

Maxine gestured.

A second blast erupted behind Loretta, unbalancing her. Then a third, and a fourth, and many more. Water pummeled Loretta in a series of explosive sprays.

And there it is! Maxine's body clenched in orgasmic release.

The world slipped away, and Maxine collapsed to the ground, crying out in pleasure.

By the time the world returned, Loretta had regained her footing and was pushing back toward the shore, a look of grim determination on her face.

Still panting, Maxine rose to her hands and knees. *Oh! Was it good for you, too?* She shook off the tremor of the afterglow, refocusing on her enemy. *Enough fun. Time to finish this.*

Maxine commanded the water to crest, building up from the other side of the pond. The wave rose, then fell upon Loretta, knocking her off her feet and slamming her body under the water.

Maxine waded into the water and pounced. She clutched a handful of Loretta's hair and held her head under.

Bubbles of panic broke the surface, and Maxine smiled, laughing. As her victim's remaining strength waned, her struggles less-ened. *Daryl's mine forever, bitch! Now, die!*

Chapter Twelve

Loretta, no! God! Through the window, Daryl watched Maxine attack Loretta. *I have to help her.* With a cry of agony, he rolled onto his side. His legs refused to work. He could only watch, helpless.

No! Please, no!

He cried out with her when the glass exploded and tore wounds in her arms and legs.

Please, Maxine, stop!

But she couldn't hear him. He didn't think she'd stop, even if she could.

"Mister Beasley?"

A pair of hands grabbed him and rolled him into a sitting position. The InfoTech woman. He tried to yell at her, but his voice barely broke above a croak. "Please help her! She's killing Loretta. You've got to help her!"

"Shush. Be still."

The woman crouched next to him, her hands gripping his shoulders like a pair of vices.

Intense heat flared at the source of her touch. Daryl gritted his teeth at the pain. Waves of agony poured through his shoulders, into his arms, down to his abdomen and legs, and up into his head.

Her words reached him from a distance. "Take my strength."

Daryl's head cleared, and he looked around from where he'd been curled up, his body and head flush with renewed energy and clarity. He folded his legs up under him and struggled to his feet.

At the same time, the stranger slumped and dropped to the carpet, her voice barely above a whisper. "You must destroy the picture frame to save Loretta. Hurry. You...don't have much time!"

Outside, Loretta fended off gusts of water that sprayed over her, disorienting her.

From the shore, Maxine motioned for a cascading wave to form behind her.

Walking on shaky legs, Daryl stepped out onto the porch and across the broken glass. As Maxine jumped out to meet Loretta at the edge of the pond, he shambled out to the yard.

His eyes scanned the shore for a weapon: a branch, a bat, anything!

The picture frame!

The frame laid in the grass, discarded, a fresh spider-web crack of breaking glass marring the surface. Clasping the frame by either side, he lifted it over his head.

He waded out into the water and closed the distance as fast as he could. The sight of Maxine, with her back to Daryl, holding Loretta under the water, propelled him forward.

With a cry of fury, he smashed the picture down over Maxine's head.

The frame exploded in a spray of glass. The fragile check fluttered down and landed on the surface of the pond.

Within moments, the decades-old paper saturated with water and deteriorated into globs of pulp.

Maxine gasped. She released Loretta and clawed at her own hair, each spasm causing a howl of pain and agony. She toppled sideways into the water.

Daryl scrambled past Maxine to reach Loretta. He grabbed a random mass of saturated cloth and yanked her up.

Loretta's head broke the surface. She coughed and gagged, struggling to breathe. She spat out water. Her hands grasped his upper arms, and he pulled her to her feet, still sputtering. "I'll kill her! I'll...Daryl! I'll..."

He pulled her close to him, so dammed relieved. He'd almost lost her, all through his own stupidity.

"Daryl, she tried; she almost..."

"I know." He kissed her forehead. "It's over. I destroyed the check. It's over, baby; you're okay, it's over."

Loretta sucked in her first full breath since surfacing and blinked, looking around as if seeing her surroundings for the first time.

They separated, but held on to each others' hands, looking down at the bleeding, crumpled mess that was once Maxine Marie.

The body quivered where it lay in the shallow edge of the pond. Fresh cuts marred her still-lovely face, arms, and legs. Rivulets of blood tainted the water beneath her. As they watched, the grimace of fury faded, replaced by a look of terror.

Loretta looked into his face. "You did that?"

Daryl shrugged. "She was killing you."

Loretta closed her eyes. Though her body was soaked, Daryl could see fresh tears cascading down and blotching her face.

"Loretta, it wasn't her. I mean, it wasn't Maxine."

The moment lingered between them, and Loretta separated her hand from his. "I know." She released his hand and turned, taking a shaky step toward the shore.

Daryl started after her, but a pathetic, croaking voice called out. "Daryl..."

Daryl stopped; a cold, bitter shudder clenched his gut.

Maxine lay, looking up at him. She reached an arm out, blood trailing from a fresh wound along her forearm. "Please, Daryl...."

Appalled, Daryl stepped back. He turned away, and his eyes

met Loretta's, who looked back with...sadness? Contempt? He couldn't tell.

Maxine continued to call. "Please, Daryl, don't...let me die...alone."

Oh, God!

He turned toward Loretta. "I can't. I can't leave her. She's dying."

"She died fifty years ago," Loretta said, disgust apparent in her voice.

"Why does that matter?" He swallowed back his anger.

She stepped toward the shore.

Daryl grabbed her forearm, stopping her. "Don't. I need you."

A look of revulsion crossed Loretta's face. "To do *what?*"

Daryl motioned toward the body. "She needs me. I need you. I know that now, more than ever. Please, she's dying. I can't do this without you."

Loretta choked back a sob. "That's not fair. I want nothing to do with this."

"Do it for me."

Loretta's look of fury withered Daryl. "You did *not* just say that to me!"

"I'm sorry." Daryl stepped back, repelled by the force of her anger. "We're running out of time, and I'm not thinking. Please, Loretta, just, please. Please help me."

His plea hovered between them.

Loretta closed her eyes. A fresh tear trickled down her face. "Fine. Go."

Together, they waded toward the crumpled body lying in the shallow water.

A spray of blood covered the front of Maxine's yellow sundress. Her bloodied hand, still reaching out blindly, dropped, sinking into the water.

Daryl scrambled toward her, kneeling down, scooping up her ice-cold body and pulling her across his lap.

Loretta sank to her knees in front of Daryl. She looked into Maxine's face.

Daryl cradled her head. "I'm here, Maxine, We're both here. Please, tell me it's not too late."

Maxine blinked, and her eyes scanned his face, traveled over his features. "Daryl...you came back." Her lips curled up in a smile.

"It's okay, Maxine. You're not alone."

Maxine's head lolled. He felt her shift under him. "She's *with* you." Her body shook.

Daryl gripped her tighter and managed to hold on, but it was like trying to keep a grip on a human-sized flopping fish. *God, maybe this was a bad idea.*

Loretta reached out and grabbed Maxine's hand. "It's okay; I'm not going to hurt you."

Loretta and Daryl held on as Maxine's body shook though a series of tremors. Just when he feared she'd break free and end up back in the water, the shaking subsided. As she settled, Maxine and Loretta locked gazes.

Maxine spoke. "You must hate me."

Loretta looked away, down toward the water. "I don't know what I'm supposed to say."

Maxine growled a response. "Don't say anything. Just hate me."

Loretta blinked. "What?"

"Hate me. Don't hate Daryl." Maxine reached out and squeezed Loretta's hand.

Loretta's eyes widened as if she wanted to cry out, and Daryl saw her fingers turn red. She said nothing.

Maxine held on and drew a deep breath. "I did it. I did *all* of it."

Loretta grimaced and pulled her hand loose. "Maxine, stop."

"He was alone...watching one of my movies, and I attacked him." Dying or not, Maxine's words toppled out of her in her haste to make her point. "That's what happened. It's not even the first time I've stolen a man. He didn't stand a chance. He'll tell you himself. I threw myself at him, tore off my shirt and—"

"Please!" Loretta grimaced. "I don't want to hear it."

"Fine, don't hear it. But hate me. It's all my fault. Do you hear me, you stupid cow?"

Loretta's face flushed red. "Stop it. I know what you're doing."

Maxine's head hung limp; her effort left her panting. "You'd still be together; you'd still be happy, if not for me. You know it. Please...just...hate me."

Loretta drew a shaky breath. "The critics were wrong about you, Maxine. You're a terrific actress when you want to be. But you can't fix this by trying to take all the blame, and you *sure* can't convince me that he did nothing wrong. Daryl has to own up to what he did, and even still..." She looked down at her own reflection. "I can't promise you what that will mean."

Maxine shook her head and rolled her eyes. "Fine. Then, just listen."

Daryl spoke up. "Please, Maxine, don't do this now."

A bitter laugh shook her body. "It's my death. I'm doing it right this time."

Maxine focused on Loretta with a sharp stare. "When you ran away from me, I..." She stopped, seeming to gather her strength. "He ...refused...to give you up. And I...made him pay. I hurt him...I...tortured him...nearly killed him. Because I knew...he loved you. Not me."

She reached out and grabbed Loretta's hand. "You. Not me.... Not...me."

"Shhh." Loretta placed the back of her other hand against Maxine's cheek. "I don't hate you. And I *do* hear you. Okay? I *do* hear you."

Daryl witnessed the entire exchange in stunned silence.

The concerned look in Loretta's eyes woke him as if from a dream. "Say goodbye," she commanded. "She's almost gone."

Daryl looked into Maxine's face.

Her eyes stared past him, out of focus. She struggled to draw a breath, her body shivering from the effort. "Thank...you."

"For what?"

She reached up to stroke the side of his face. He tried to

ignore the cold, eerie chill of her touch. "For letting me see...*me*...through your eyes..."

"You're still beautiful, Maxine."

She smiled. "You're sweet." She struggled to draw one last breath. "Fight for her, Daryl..."

Daryl choked back a sob. "I will."

Her hand rose toward his face. "Tell me..." Her voice failed her. Her hand dropped into the lapping water.

He leaned forward and kissed her forehead. "I love you."

"Be ...mine..." Her head slumped and fell against his shoulder as dead weight.

He ran a hand through her matted hair and wept, looking down at her peaceful face one last time, the smooth, pale skin marred by ugly red gashes.

A moment later, her body dissolved in his arms, and he huddled in the chilled water, drenched and shivering.

All his strength had abandoned him. But, as he slumped into the water, Loretta's arms wrapped around him and pulled him close, saving him just as everything began to fade to black.

That was good, Daryl thought because he had no strength to save himself.

Chapter Thirteen

COMFORTING ARMS ENCIRCLED HIM. He stared up into the face of an angel, a majestic figure, her skin aglow, her head encircled by a radiant red halo. Her eyes pierced him with blasts of healing comfort.

"Mister Beasley?"

The vision dissolved, and Daryl found himself staring at the InfoTech lady who wasn't from InfoTech, her red hair red but no longer radiant, her skin no longer glowing, and a look of businesslike concern on her stoic face.

Where am I? He looked down to find himself adrift in her arms, his wet, shivering body cradled against her.

He looked down at the pond, now several inches beneath him. "Where's Loretta?"

"Inside, safe and sound, Mister Beasley. She pulled you to the shore, but couldn't get you inside."

"And you can?"

An amused smile cracked her poker face. "For a few feet, Mister Beasley, just enough to get you into your room."

"You're...carrying me?"

"I can't think of any other way to get you into the apartment, but I'm open to suggestions." Daryl weighed every bit of 225 lbs. A few days ago, he would have said it was impossible for this skinny woman to carry him by herself.

Then again, his definition of "impossible" had shifted considerably over the last two days.

As they approached the porch, Daryl saw two men dressed in black, already standing on the porch, watching them approach. Between the two of them, they held a huge roll of construction grade clear plastic.

One of the men stepped forward, holding his arms out toward Daryl. "Ma'am?"

The woman shook her head, and the man backed down. From the look on his face, he wasn't surprised at her refusal for help. The woman snapped off orders. "Seal off the opening, as quickly and discreetly as you can. I want this door replaced, good as new, twenty-four hours at the latest. In the meantime, send a couple of men to the surrounding apartments. Find out if anyone saw anything." The authority in her voice could have spurred Daryl to action if he were not already so weak.

"Yes, ma'am!"

As they stepped past, Daryl watched, slack-jawed, over her shoulder. Men closed in behind her, spreading the plastic across the patio door opening. One man began tearing off duct tape from a large roll.

"Oh, my God, is he okay?" Loretta's voice drew his attention forward.

The woman released Daryl's legs and set his feet gently on the linoleum. The aroma of chicken soup heating up on the stove caused his stomach to growl.

Loretta stood before him wearing his Mister Spock T-shirt and a pair of his sweats that hung baggy on her. He saw the reflections of medicinal goo on the fresh cuts covering her face. Her leg bulged, presumably from a wrapping beneath the loose sweats. Someone had taped a white pad to the nasty cut on Loretta's cheek.

"He needs to get out of these clothes and into bed."

Loretta was there, next to him.

"Are you okay?"

Loretta extended her arm across his shoulders. "Compared to you? Peachy. Hold on to me. Let's get you to bed."

Daryl shook his head. "I don't know if I can—"

"You should be better than you were," said the woman. "Maxine's no longer affecting you, Mister Stevens, and you should still have some residual strength left. If you try, I think you can walk."

Loretta stepped to his side.

Daryl braced himself against her. He found that, with her help, he could indeed hobble to his room.

A couple of minutes later, Daryl was pulling the soaked polo shirt up over his head while Loretta searched through his dresser drawer. "Don't you own one pair of pajamas?" She sighed. "Something your grandmother gave you for Christmas, with Snoopy or Tweety on them?"

"You know me better than that. I'd have worn something like that loud and proud."

She laughed.

Daryl took this as a good sign.

"Ah, here's a nice, loose shirt. Just drop your shirt. I'll get it."

The shirt hit the floor with a wet sloshing sound. Loretta turned toward him, holding a pair of sweat pants and one of his favorite t-shirts with the image of D'lenn from *Babylon 5*.

She helped him unbutton his soaked jeans, pried off the rest of his clothes, and sat him down on the edge of the bed.

With quiet efficiency, she redressed him and pulled the covers back so he could lie down.

He sat through her ministration but, as she tucked the covers under his chin, he couldn't take it anymore. "Loretta, I'm sorry about—"

"I don't want to talk about it."

"Loretta, I chose you."

She glared at him. Fresh tears sprang into her eyes. She turned away. Moments later, in the near-darkness, he heard her weeping quietly.

She spoke as if she forced each word out. "You ...don't get points for...picking your girlfriend...over your fuck fantasy."

"But Loretta, I wouldn't—"

"Shut up, Daryl." She pounded a fist against the top of his dresser drawer. In spite of his fatigue, the action made him jump.

"Stupid!" she spat. "Loyal Loretta, brave Loretta." She scooped the soaked clothing into her arms. "But it's all bullshit. I love you too much to let you go. And I don't know if that's loyalty, or stupidity. And I'm *not* brave, not in the least. I'm just scared to death of facing life without you."

She opened the door, stepped through, and slammed it shut, leaving Daryl alone in the dark to stew in his misery.

LORETTA STUMBLED INTO THE HALLWAY, and, as she passed the hamper, she dropped the sopping clothes into it. Out in the great room, Rebecca spoke into her cell phone. She noted the plastic barrier against the far wall, already taped along four sides to keep the air in. *Look at her. Efficient. So very efficient.*

"Thanks, keep checking." Rebecca pocketed her phone and turned toward her.

I need a sympathetic listener, and Rebecca's the only one I can talk to about this.

"Looks like we lucked out. Some tenant on the other side of the pond reported hearing a shattering noise, but no one saw anything. So this," Rebecca motioned toward the plastic hanging across the patio, "was officially a fluke wind-gust. And fully covered by Daryl's renter's insurance. Lucky him."

Loretta rolled her eyes. "Is that really going to work?"

Rebecca approached the stove. "Yes." She grabbed the spoon in the saucepan and stirred the contents. "Soup's almost done. Hey, I know the paramedics checked you out, but I want you to let them do it again."

The idea of leaving terrified her. "No. I need to stay here."

Rebecca's hand landed, feather-light, on Loretta's shoulder. "I know, but I don't want to find out they left any glass behind. Infections can be serious."

"Let me get some soup in him first. And make sure it stays down."

Rebecca nodded. "I understand. How's your leg?"

Loretta winced, but patted the fresh gauze wrapping bulging from underneath the sweatpants. "I'll live."

"Oh, Daryl's paperwork from his doctor has already been faxed to InfoTech. As far as they're concerned, he's being treated for a nasty flu bug that will keep him down for another couple of days. But the important thing is HR has their paperwork."

Loretta nodded. "That's good, because without a good excuse, he was already in trouble with his supervisor. But why wouldn't the hospital have contacted them sooner?"

Rebecca shrugged. "Clearly, they originally sent the paperwork to the wrong fax number."

Loretta studied Rebecca's face, in awe over the personal sacrifice she'd made. Somehow, for several precious minutes, Rebecca willingly gave up her control, her strength, to Daryl. She'd trusted him to do what had to be done, and gave him an opportunity to make it right. The implications of that act spoke far louder than words.

Out loud, Loretta said, "You are *way* too efficient at this."

Rebecca smiled. "Your tax dollars at work."

"That's not what I mean. You do this a lot."

Rebecca's expression turned serious. "I can't comment on that."

"I know. And soon, you'll have to go."

"Well, yes."

The silence lingered between them.

Rebecca met Loretta's gaze. "Look. What I can tell you is," she motioned to the room around her as if embracing the entire scenario, "this was pretty extreme, even compared to other episodes I've dealt with. This isn't something I want to encounter again, anytime soon."

"And how are *you* doing, Rebecca?"

Rebecca shrugged. "I think we're about wrapped up, once we make sure—"

"That's not what I mean, and you know it." On an impulse, Loretta reached out and gave Rebecca a tentative hug, noting how Rebecca's body stiffened as she did so. "You sacrificed a lot for me, and for Daryl. On a very personal level. I'm going to miss you."

Rebecca's fingers tapped against Loretta's shoulder. "All in a day's work." Her voice sounded professional, but with a hint of a tremble. "It was nothing, compared to what you've both gone through. It's just what I have to do."

Loretta began scooping out the soup into a smaller bowl using Daryl's ladle. Actually, Loretta had purchased both the saucepan and ladle months ago. "This is not just another case, and you are not just another federal contractor. I get that. And I get that you can't talk about it. I just hope that you're taking care of yourself."

Rebecca nodded. "Thank you."

LORETTA OPENED THE BEDROOM DOOR. The brightness from the hall lit up the room, and she could see sadness on Daryl's face. He lay where she'd left him, still covered to his neck in the blankets.

Upon the door opening, Daryl struggled back onto his elbows.

Loretta set the tray on the dresser, adjusted Daryl's pillow so he could sit up, retrieved the tray, and placed it on the bed between them.

"There you are, snug as a bug in a rug."

Daryl smiled, but said nothing. Gently, she dipped the spoon into the yellow-green broth and brought it to his lips.

For the next several minutes, silence hung between them. She continued to feed him, first just the broth, and then, he began to slurp the noodles with vigor.

When he'd drained the bowl, Loretta dabbed his mouth with a napkin. Finally, she broke the silence. "How do you feel?"

"Much better. My stomach still hurts, but it's just hunger now."

"Good. We'll take care of that. Do you want some more?"

"Please."

"I'll get you some." She started to rise.

"Loretta?"

"Hmm?"

"Are we..." He hesitated. "Are we okay?"

"Oh, I don't know, Daryl."

Daryl swallowed and said nothing.

Loretta released a strange sound, like a combination laugh and sob. "I mean, you are...*such* a geek." She shook her head, but flashed him a kind smile. "But you're *my* geek, and I...I love you very much."

"I love you, too. I didn't realize how much until all this happened."

Loretta retrieved the empty bowl of soup from the tray and left, leaving Daryl to rest easy.

The End

About the Author

R.J. Sullivan's novel *Haunting Blue* (2010) is an edgy paranormal thriller and the first book of the adventures of punk girl Fiona "Blue" Shaefer and her boyfriend Chip Farren. *Haunting Obsession (2012)* and *Virtual Blue* (2013) continue the paranormal thriller series. R.J.'s short stories have been featured in such acclaimed collections as *Dark Faith Invocations* by Apex Books and *Vampires Don't Sparkle*. These stories were compiled in R.J.'s 2015 collection *Darkness with a Chance of Whimsy*. Revised editions of these titles were released by DarkWhimsy Books in 2020.

Commanding the Red Lotus (2016) collects three space opera tales in the tradition of Andre Norton and Gene Roddenberry. New titles to the series are forthcoming from Hydra Publications.

rjsullivanfiction.com

Haunting Obsession
Elegant Paper Dolls

Maxine and Loretta
gorgeous glossy color book
4" figures, 10 costume changes!
$5! Sexy and Cheap!

Order exclusively from
RJSullivanFiction.com or
at personal appearances.

Renderings by Nell Williams,
NellWilliams.com

The Original Paranormal Thrills by R.J. Sullivan...

...Revised Editions by 

RJSullivanFiction.com

Also Available
in Audiobook

Narrated by
Danielle Muething

DanielleMuething.wixsite.com/mysite/about

Travel Through Time and Space with R J Sullivan

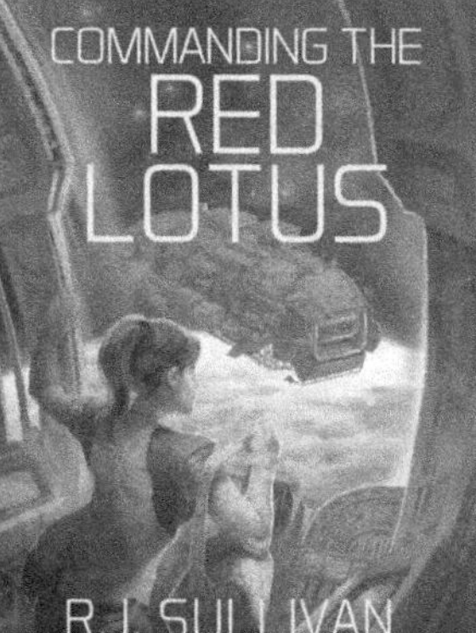

**RJSullivanFiction.com
or Amazon.com**

This book is part of an author-cooperative urban fantasy universe. Characters created by E. Chris Garrison (including Skye MacLeod and the Transit King) and R.J. Sullivan (including "Blue" Shaefer and Rebecca Burton) interact in a shared world. For example, Chris's Transit King appears in R.J.'s Haunting Obsession, while R.J.'s Rebecca Burton lends a hand in Chris's Mean Spirit. So if you love what you just read and want the entire story, here's a handy guide and timeline to:

The Skye-Blue-niverse

Haunting Blue by R.J. Sullivan *
Four 'Til Late by E. Chris Garrison**
Haunting Obsession by R.J. Sullivan
Sinking Down by E. Chris Garrison**
Blue Spirit by E. Chris Garrison
Me and the Devil by E. Chris Garrison**
Virtual Blue by R.J. Sullivan*
Restless Spirit by E. Chris Garrison
Mean Spirit by E. Chris Garrison

*Also part of The Collected Adventures of Blue Shaefer by R.J. Sullivan
**Part of the Road Ghosts Omnibus by E. Chris Garrison

Enter the Skye-Blue-niverse at:

**https://sillyhatbooks.com/
and
https://rjsullivanfiction.com/**

www.ingramcontent.com/pod-product-compliance
Lightning Source LLC
Chambersburg PA
CBHW060805210726
48292CB00013B/1771